D1168465

DATE DUE

TYCOONERY

TYCOONERY

Roger Smith

VERSO
London • New York

First published by Verso 2012

The moral rights of the author have been asserted

1 3 5 7 9 10 8 6 4 2

Verso
UK: 6 Meard Street, London W1F 0EG
US: 20 Jay Street, Suite 1010, Brooklyn, NY 11201

www.versobooks.com

Verso is the imprint of New Left Books

ISBN-13: 978-1-84467-898-3

British Library Cataloguing in Publication Data
A catalogue record for this book is available from the British Library

Library of Congress Cataloging-in-Publication Data
Smith, Roger, 1937–
Tycoonery / by Roger Smith.
p. cm.
ISBN 978-1-84467-898-3 (hardback : alk. paper) –
ISBN 978-1-84467-937-9 (ebook : alk. paper)
1. Businessmen–Fiction. 2. Real estate development–Fiction.
3. Man-woman relationships–Fiction. I. Title.
PR6119.M5813T93 2012
823'.92–dc23
2012018388

Typeset in Electra by MJ Gavan
Printed and bound in the US by Maple Vail

To Daisy, Jonny, Molly and Betty

Any similarity to characters living or dead is
merely evidence of the times we live in.

ROGER SMITH
Tycoonery
a novel

Chapter 1

1971

I puzzle them at the Ministry of Employment and Productivity. Not with my demands, which are modest to be sure, and involve no more than to be allowed to collect on a Thursday the paltry allowance that the welfare state allots me.

My appearance too is unexceptional, my clothing neat though worn, my nails short but clean, my chin shaven, my ears free of wax, and my underwear as stain-free as can be expected of a bachelor of thirty-five, living alone in reduced circumstances in one room in Paddington, a ten-minute walk from the launderette, and nourished by an eclectic diet.

My manner to them is neither servile nor proud, but professional in the way acquired by one accustomed to queuing and waiting and taking.

In fact they are puzzled by my qualifications, which include eight assorted subjects at ordinary level, three at advanced and a first-class degree in English language and literature at the University of Oxford, not to mention a PhD on Trollope.

They are more than embarrassed, I suspect, by their inability to find a position for me commensurate with such qualifications, and since I resigned from my position as lecturer in English some five years ago and have not the slightest intention of returning to it, they receive little co-operation on these matters from me. In short, I have no desire to participate in the degrading activities that pass as gainful employment in this our society.

'Have you thought of advertising?' they say to me periodically, more out of hope than conviction.

'Indeed I have and my answer must be in the negative.' I then explain to them the harlotry of that occupation, suited only to charlatans and purveyors of falsehood.

'But surely you want to get on?' enquires Mr Jackson, a red-faced man in horn-rimmed glasses and a shiny herringbone suit, who always smells of carbolic soap. His enquiry is not without concern or pathos, coming from a man whose very existence, for its sheer drudgery and awe-inspiring boredom, must negate for all time the plausibility of the concept 'getting on'.

'If you speak of the dehumanising and alienating confines of the capitalist system then my answer must be no.' I reply with more conviction than you might find necessary in dealing with a functionary of the state.

'Then I'm afraid there's nothing we can offer you this

week,' he says, handing me over the money, which I count scrupulously, before nodding to him with a smile and disappearing through the blistered swing doors out into the carbon monoxide-laden air of the streets.

That particular Thursday, the one of which I write, the one when it all began, I purchased forty cigarettes from the corner store, noticing on one of the dusty shelves between the Kiwi boot polish and the sliced bread a small brown bottle which read, confidently and unequivocally, 'SLOAN'S KILLS PAIN'. I could not help thinking with a certain ironic pleasure, 'I've tried everything else. Who knows?'

It buoyed my spirits and I sang as I walked up to my room, hardly aware of the glum and dank paintwork, the curious pervasive smell of kippers and the gas bill ominous in its sandy envelope lying snugly amid the pile of free samples that flow in never-ending profusion through my indifferent letter box. Lighting a cigarette and taking the *Telegraph*, I made my way to the lavatory to defecate and chuckle over the more preposterous and patriotic statements of this ruling class organ. I settled down for fifteen minutes of pleasure, heralded, much to my delight, by a crisp and resonant fart.

Puzzled experience has taught me that there is some uncanny connection between the movement of my bowels and the telephone service, for almost every time I settle astride the confident and purposeful chinaware of the Sanitas, the usual gloomy silence of my room is shattered by

3

a call. It always throws me in confusion. There I sit, my trousers round my ankles, my stained pants accusing me, my arse sticky with turd, suspended in panic while the electronic bell invites me.

Sometimes I have wedged my rectum with Andrex and hobbled across the floor to the recently installed slot-type phone (the more homely model was removed after a protracted court case involving non-payment of bill) only to be greeted on panting arrival with an abrupt and strangled silence indicating that the caller had hung up. I call this experience 'effort unrewarded'. The result is intense anxiety, for not only has the sensual pleasure of crapping been curtailed, vandalised one might almost say, but I am now in a state of unsatiated curiosity as to the identity of the caller, and having few acquaintances, who call at any hour of the day or night whenever it enters their heads and in absolute disregard for the inconvenience it might cause me, the telephone can only mean that a new experience is about to enter my somewhat uneventfully chaotic life.

Indeed, you might well ask, disapprovingly, why one in my position who has so resolutely broken with the customary preoccupations of bourgeois life should bother himself with such trivial questions. You might even wonder why I still maintain in my flat at unnecessary expense and obvious inconvenience so peremptory and demanding an instrument of modern life as the telephone. Is it a sign of immaturity?

Undoubtedly it is, but there is a rather more practical if neurotic explanation.

Living as I do on my own, it has crossed my mind not infrequently that an occasion could well arise when I am stricken by one of the multitudinous viruses that thrive and multiply in our atmosphere. I have visualised my death at the hand or tail of one of these voracious microbes, my life ebbing away in solitude, my body weak from undernourishment, and the gathering half-pint milk bottles at the door the only visible symptoms of my imminent demise.

It is some comfort to me to know that in the event of such catastrophe I could crawl, albeit weakly, to the phone and dial 999. It is one of the few institutions I have faith in. Perhaps my day of judgement will find them wanting and though my faith might well be the last surviving remnant of earlier primitive belief in mythology, I cling to it nevertheless.

Meanwhile, at eleven-thirty on that Thursday morning as I sat astride the water closet, browsing through the letter columns of the *Daily Telegraph*, my face flushed from my purposeful efforts, the cheeks of my arse warm on the woodwork, as if on cue confusion was announced by the shrill imperious tones of the telephone. I waited a customary five seconds, as irritations welled, then nipping a turd in the bud, placed the *Telegraph* on the linoleum floor, stuffed three sheets of carefully folded Andrex into my orifice, and shuffled as if in a sack race into the stale disorder of my bed sitting room.

Bent at the knees, and leaning at a thirty-degree angle from the waist, I picked up the receiver and announced my name in a tone hopefully confident enough to conceal the fact that I stood there in a state of ridiculous vulnerability.

'George Timmins,' I said and cleared my throat.

'Hello, George. How are you?'

Certain people are possessed of such unshakeable confidence in their own identity that the very chore of announcing their name seems a preposterous irrelevance. Such people are a source of considerable irritation to me. I have been known to replace the receiver on its cradle without uttering a sound. Only one other kind of person irritates me more. They conduct themselves on telephones in exactly the same lofty fashion but so distinctive is their voice that even after considerable periods of absence it is immediately recognisable. Such is the voice of David Adler.

It has a light fruitiness, modulated like an actor's, caressing, sleepy, sensual, as if he has just woken up and you are the first person he thought of. (At eleven-thirty he probably was still in bed.) The flat London vowels only add to its persuasiveness, with its accentuated lilt, soft, slurred, flowing. It is curious to think that an accidental or genetic arrangement of the vocal chords, assiduously cultivated, can afford the basis of so much worldly success. The listener felt privileged to eavesdrop on David Adler's intimate aloofness. And one look into those soft, large, grey-green eyes trebled the honour.

'Who is that speaking?' I asked sharply.

An indulgent sigh brushed its silky way along the impartial wires. 'It's David,' implying who else could it be, and indeed, who else could it have been? 'I'd like to see you.'

I had anticipated the request. In eleven years it had come some five times before. It usually signified some change in his material progress, a new flat, a more expensive car, a suite of offices more opulent, leather-bound and automated than the previous ones. And on five occasions I had shaved, changed my shirt and cleaned my teeth, then boarded the appropriate means of public transport to place myself in, or around, or by or outside the particular acquisition that he wanted to draw my attention to. Glumly I had nodded my indifferent approval, simulating a response only when he threw a glance at me. I would prod a button, or finger some paintwork, or pat a cushion. 'Very nice. Very nice.' He always seemed unperturbed by my palpable lack of enthusiasm. Indeed, it was questionable whether he was even aware of my presence, so self-absorbed did he seem in the obviously sensual pleasure of ownership, as if the motor car or room, whatever it happened to be, was not just the product of arduous human labour, an arrangement of brick or steel welded together by the labourer's sweat, but had some kind of magical property of its own that conferred upon him a special privilege. The grey-green eyes glistened, reflecting in miniature the new icon, as if by some secret process of transubstantiation he had ingested it into his very being. And though the pleasure was shortlived like all mystical experiences (by the time he had helped me into my coat and thrust two crisp fivers into my damp and eager hands, the magic had already passed and he was bored) it had answered, nevertheless, some deep-seated spiritual need.

That I should be required to act as witness to this communion often gave me cause to ponder, usually at night as I lay back on my fetid sheets, my feet snug in their socks, steamy from the day's labour, my right hand fondling affably my much abused and easily amused member. At such times the darkness around me, the raucous noises of the streets reassuring me, lying in wait to answer the call of my capricious libido, a box of Kleenex at the alert on the bedside table, tissue memorials to the nonconceived, between those moments of lights out and masturbation I muse over life in a kind of suspended animation. It came to me on one such occasion that David needed me to allay his guilt. And if this seems an admittedly banal explanation, no less true for its banality, it has a less analytic corollary which avers that he needs my presence BECAUSE NO ONE ELSE CÁN DEFINE HIS PROGRESS LIKE ME.

Confusing? Perhaps. But when I make it known that I am thirty-five and David is thirty-four and that we have known each other for thirty of those voracious and life-consuming years, then perhaps my meaning is clearer. We began our relationship at the ages of five and four, confronting each other in check shirts and grey flannel knickers: he dug his grubby nails into my face and drew blood. For two years he dictated the course of my history with those nails and, when they proved insufficient, with studded boots that showered sparks as he slid along the way, until, somewhat uncharacteristically I now concede, while grappling with him in the street, he predictably clawing at my face, I seized his head and banged it hard three times on the grey stone pavement. My surprise action stunned him more than the kerb stone, and from then on a dialectical change took place as the Hegelians will have it, a change from quantity (three blows) into quality (his submission). I had negated his thesis.

Since that time he has tried to negate my negation. His rivalry took on more sophisticated guise, masking his deep-rooted respect for the kerb stone.

'Well I'm rather busy just now.'

He laughed. 'You're probably lying around in that grotty flat. Look, come on over. I'll give you lunch. You probably need a decent meal. And I need to talk to you.'

He was right about the lunch, and he usually gave a good lunch. But there were other considerations. Admittedly five summonses in fifteen years is hardly being at his beck and call, but why should I submit to his overture?

You will remember I had been called from the lavatory seat, and that I stood, my trousers round my ankles, inclined some thirty degrees to the perpendicular. Such a stance afforded me a view of the nether regions of a chest of drawers that stood by the telephone. Perhaps it was first the sunlight that attracted my attention for it highlighted a layer of dust of wondrous texture, like a rich extravagant carpet that had gathered beneath the battered mahogany of disorderly drawers. Next I chanced upon a crumpled Kleenex, thrown aside no doubt after a night of particularly reckless passion; no more than nine inches to the left of the discarded tissue was a small piece of fruit cake, and nibbling at the said piece of cake, its eye black and provocative, was a small furry mouse. Usually I take such manifestations in my living room as a matter of course, as an inevitable hazard faced by those who live in a state of disarray and dirt. But a combination of certain things, the telephone call, the stirrings of some dead rivalry, but most of all the extreme exposure of my condition, trousers at ankles, Y-fronts at calves, penis bared to the elements and, worse, to the needle-boned tooth of my rodent intruder, and (some homosexual anxiety erupting?) three sheets of Andrex plugged in my bum, all conspired to make me break out in a cold and shivering sweat. I lurched for my trousers and dragged them up my goose-pimpled legs, whose hairs were rising like a field of wheat. I banged the chest of drawers with my elbow, which did nothing to disrupt the early lunching and munching of my unwanted guest. A sharp kick seemed to make him only more resolved to stay. It was a conflict of wills, and already the beast of two inch length proved more determined than I.

At this point the forgotten receiver was saying, 'Get a taxi and come over.'

'Right away,' I shouted, 'right away,' conceding ignomini-ous defeat to both mouse and man.

I hastily replaced the telephone, rushed back to the lavatory, where anxiety moved my bowels to extravagant proportions. Wiped, washed, coated and hatted, I left my apartment without so much as a glance at that part of my home now requisitioned by an alien creature.

Chapter 2

The street calmed my quivering nervous system. The sky was a pale autumnal blue and the weak sharp-rimmed sun was lethargically reaching its highest meridional point. It was a time of the year when the season seems to brace itself with a kind of expectancy before lurching into the bleak shrouds of winter. My stride took up its rhythm and my open sandals rediscovered a spring.

As I descended the escalator to the Bakerloo line, the swim suit – or bathing costume, as we used to call it – ads seemed unusually provocative. Those lithe, blonde and suggestively sleazy girls, thrusting forth their delectable crotches, must have unnerved many a man, but such is the hold of our puritanism that only on one occasion have I seen anyone give vent to his natural impulses, and that late at night, when a squat bowler-hatted man emerged from the train to the foot of the stairs, placed his hat and umbrella in his left hand, and with his right unzipped his flies, and lying across the moving rubber banister, wanked his way from poster to poster, reaching a sudden, ecstatic if silent climax some ten yards from the top, which he directed precisely and methodically into his bowler hat. He was arrested at the ticket barrier.

My new-discovered mood, the empty train (curiously there is nothing more liberating, more likely to give a sense of well-being and contentment, than an empty compartment rattling its way through the depths of London at midday), turned my thoughts to David and, because they are inextricably linked, my childhood.

It haunts me with an exaggerated nostalgia. The years since lack that sharp clarity of focus with which I can still evoke places, colours, feelings, fantasies, new pleasures, the secrecy of a child's world of cowboys and Indians, camps in the ferns, identities assumed. Whether that sense of extremes that I recall at thirty-five is illusory I no longer know, but wartime summers stretched on into double summertime and winters seem crisp with snow and sledges. I discovered the dark thrill of the cinema and the names and faces of the stars, the impossible celluloid girls that I still yearn for, woven now into a thread of unrealisable fantasies that pulls at today's experience with a tug of disappointment or permanent regret. And David shared that with me; for we grew up in the same town.

Trowbridge Spa marked its growth across the years in a crablike movement north. Some time at the turn of the nineteenth century some passing nobleman discovered a spring five miles outside the Norman town of Trowbridge in Kent, and the spa became a popular health resort. The water is sharp, cold with a tang of iron. The well still exists, though the old woman who sells it at a penny a glass is far removed from the fashionable Regency circles who once flocked there, and only a small cluster of elegantly proportioned shops and houses bear testimony to their past existence. By 1940 when I first arrived, an evacuee from the blitz, the town sprawled in different architectural shock waves out from the nucleus of the spa, up the hill in early Victorian, along the straight in late Victorian and finally merged with lush Kent countryside in a scattering of thirties speculative. To the east it was fringed by a common of coarse grass and fern, bracken, a profusion of trees, and an exotic outburst of sandstone rocks, carved by generations of lovers and trippers, their names and pledges worn away by wind and rain and the feet of a thousand children. For me, this seemingly endless stretch of common land with its names – Devil's Dyke, Donkey Stand, High Rocks, the Sandpit – provided the location for a million dreams and celluloid games, where the fearless bandits George and Dave lurked and plotted, the two steely-eyed sheriffs patrolled, the twin fighter pilots purged the sky of the sun. There was little that could not be righted or frighted by us terrible two.

Children have a great sense of the hierarchy of age and my one slender year of seniority conferred on me all sorts of privileges of leadership. It was assumed that David should play Will Scarlet to my Robin Hood, Ginger to my Just William, deputy to my sheriff. That one year seemed to make an enormous difference to us. It separated us at school, even at Sunday school, and later sent me in new cap and blazer to the grammar school while he remained with the infants. But education wasn't the real business of living and it was after school hours, or in the seemingly endless summer holidays, that our relationship developed, when the games took over and we made flesh and blood the heroes of our books and comics, while above us in the skies planes first etched out their battles in tracer shells and then gave way to the spluttering engines of the doodlebug.

To us the war seemed only an extension of our games, its menace only glimpsed on the trembling knees of parents in air raid shelters when it was said that incendiary bombs were falling on the town like fireworks. The next day brought the thrill of searching for shrapnel in craters, for cartridge cases, unused shells. Later the war brought American soldiers who ran off with our girls, it was said, and showered us with gum and candy from their jeeps. It brought glimpses of the enemy too, cheerful Italian prisoners of war in green uniforms who waved at us and whistled from their trucks.

And then the radio announced it was all over and there were Union Jacks and bunting and fireworks and bonfires on which Hitler was burnt as the guy. And a strange man who turned out to be my father came home, and David's father arrived having spent forty-eight hours in the Mediterranean on a plank. But after their leave was over and the uniforms put away, they went back to their jobs and found the same old drudgery. The promises of the 'White Cliffs of Dover' had a hollow ring.

But for us there were pantomimes at Christmas, and the principal girl to love, and the radio comics and the catch phrases and the dreadful empty songs and the cinema and Esther Williams and Sonja Henie and Humphrey Bogart and Gene Kelly and …

Need I go on? Those drab, grey, heartbreaking, defeated years are forever touched with the romance of childhood.

When I was twelve the family moved back to London. It was after all our original place of domicile, and it was only Hitler who had sent us scurrying to the sticks, though there was no doubt in my mother's mind that it was a temporary arrangement and as if to prove it, throughout four years of global warfare and three years of ensuing peace, the front room carpet was turned upside down, its pink fern-like pattern to the floor. She was waiting for a home of her own where the full rosy glory of the Wilton could be displayed; to her way of thinking the two rooms that we occupied in Trowbridge Spa did not qualify for that status. My mother incidentally is an interesting woman, but since she is not particularly central to this story (do I hear the Freudians chortle? All right, in a narrative sense) I intend only to allude to her from time to time whenever for the sake of historical authenticity it is necessary. But home being where the heart is for those who don't have the financial wherewithal for a mortgage, we were dependent on the good if bureaucratic offices of the Lewisham

Borough Council, as it then was, for accommodation, and lists being lists and long with it, and bomb damage being somewhat extensive in the metropolis, it took three more years of agitation on my determined mother's part, and three years of desperation on my father's, who worked in a factory in Shoreditch, sleeping in dusty lodgings during the week, and three years of reprieve for me, already advancing up the ladder of success and now attending the local grammar school, before an enormous pantechnicon, larger by far than anything we had ever lived in or were likely to, engulfed our few bits of protected and polished furniture and deposited them on the pavements of Sydenham. To those familiar with the geography of London, it would be superfluous to point out that Sydenham is almost as far removed from Shoreditch as it is possible to be and necessitated my father getting out of his bed, wherein he had slumped the night before, unconscious after overtime, at the hell-ridden hour of five-thirty; it is also many bus journeys away from the nearest school and, as far as my young vision could take in, practically everything else. Nevertheless we had a home and a bathroom for the first time in our lives and we were no longer classed as provincials.

The greatest loss for me was David. I was now in a large sprawling and incomprehensible city, at a hateful new school and without my closest friend. We wrote letters and looked forward to the holidays, but letters never reflect the real unstated nuances of relationships; rather they add a self-conscious element, the role of letter writer obtrudes, and as two boys who had entered the trap of prestige education, our words soon echoed the pretentiousness of misspelt French and schoolboy Latin. A new rivalry emerged and when we met again almost a year later it was this rivalry that created the context of our relationship. We faced each other like contenders, cagey, weighing the other up behind awkward smiles.

David had grown too and was now three inches at least taller than me. His voice had broken or was in the process of breaking and would make sudden violent and unpredictable shifts from basso profundo to strangled squeak. I still felt a boy and the privilege of that one year's seniority seemed fraudulent in a soprano. At the swimming bath changing rooms that solid meaty and hairy thing between his legs had something of substance, of manhood. Shivering, my eyes full of chlorine, I rubbed ferociously with my towel at the little bit of string in my thighs, hoping magically that the friction might rub it into rope-like size. He said nothing but contented himself with rubbing his back easily and lazily like an athlete, knowing that my eyes were transfixed by the dark heavy metamorphosed growth of his prick.

I countered by being metropolitan, for what did such arbitrary physical differences make to an inhabitant of one of the oldest and largest cities in the world, which placed at my feet theatres, cinemas, music, art galleries. Though as yet I had only penetrated the local Odeon I felt I had a right to this cultural heritage, the history, the architecture, the latest in fashion. The city was beginning to emerge from its postwar gloom. Soon the streets would be neon-lit like Broadway.

'When you come to London,' I said, 'I must take you to Soho. They have prostitutes there waiting on the streets to be had.'

We parted and though the letters were more sporadic they continued intermittently. We saw each other in the summer holidays. At school it became clear that I was the bright boy, while in Trowbridge Spa, still that year behind, David notched up his successes. I went through the examination tide, O level, A level, and then the postman brought the news that I had won an open scholarship to New College, Oxford.

We celebrated, the pair of us, in Soho. A spaghetti bolognese and espresso coffee. Jazz was having its revival and skiffle too. We wandered about the streets eyeing the whores, November breath steaming out of us, wearing duffel coats and cheese cutters. And two pints later he said, 'Do you fancy a whore?' How can you look at your best friend and closest rival and say that the idea terrifies the life out of you, that your bowels have turned to soup even at the suggestion, that your knees have become putty and your scrotum is as tight as a baby's fist? So I blew out some smoke from my Senior Service and laughed, 'Do you?'

He shrugged. 'I might do.'

'You wouldn't dare.'

He stubbed out his cigarette, got up from the table, flicked his shoulders inside his duffel and left by the saloon entrance.

I could see him through the window. He approached a tart standing theatrically under a street lamp and said something to her, then they went off together.

I rolled the silver paper of the cigarette pack into a tight, humiliated ball and drank another half of bitter. Then he reappeared, his cheese cutter set a little more jauntily, but otherwise unruffled. He sat down without saying anything and lit another cigarette.

'Was it all right?' I asked.

He sniffed and scratched the back of his neck. 'It was all right,' he said.

A year later he won an open scholarship to Christ's, Cambridge. He was seventeen and a half.

The years at university produced the final rift. Oxford seemed to me at eighteen an enchanted if intimidating place. I could think of nowhere else I would rather work or live, peaceful, secure, beautiful, learned. I decided early on that I would like to teach there, and addressed myself to the realisation of that task. It meant a great deal of hard work, burrowing in libraries, missing most of the activities that others pursued, occupying the shadows and the periphery. Many thought I was dull. And certainly I must have appeared so in contrast to the flamboyant reports that came from Cambridge. Like everything else, David seized Cambridge by the scruff of the neck. He acted, edited the university paper, threw parties, laid upper middle-class girls who threw themselves at his proletarian feet. I went once to a party he gave there, and got the impression that he was embarrassed to see me, and indeed it was obvious to me and to him that I did not fit into his world. He ignored me most of the evening, and I felt that I owed my place there yet again to his need to demonstrate his superiority. I returned to Oxford feeling rather flat.

Three years passed quickly enough and in the summer of 57 I took my degree. Surprisingly, he sent a letter wishing me well and suggested that we might meet in London. Three weeks later we had dinner in a small Italian restaurant. He said, 'What are you going to do?'

I told him of my plans to teach, to write a thesis, to stay in Oxford.

He leant back in his chair and grinned. He said, 'You're a cunt, all that academic stuff is bollocks. When I get my degree I'm going into property. You can make a fortune at it. I want to make a lot of money. I want a big luxury flat, a wardrobe full of clothes, a fast car, holidays abroad, and as many good-looking birds as I can screw.'

If, as a statement of faith, it was calculated to shock me, it did just that. I knew then that we had absolutely nothing in common, that we remained absolute opposites. And if tenacity of purpose is considered a sterling quality, then sterling qualities he had, for from that day he remained loyal to a twenty-year-old's creed.

Chapter 3

Such were my memories as I left the underground train at Knightsbridge and turned right into Sloane Street, threading my way among the middle-class hordes who congregate there, exchanging their ill-gotten and ill-deserved gains for the domestic booty found in the many and expensive stores that line the pavements. At noon the womenfolk predominate, dressed in a style that is set by the reigning monarch, gloved, handbagged and hatted, their middle-aged sagging bellies rumbling with flatulence in rubber corsets, their shoulders drooping from the weight of pendulous dugs, and their faces, oh, so bitter and defeated, and arrogant. Where have all their mouths gone, curled into their gums every one? Were they ever young, were they ever pretty, did they ever fuck? Did those shrill, near-hysterical voices, aimed now at shop assistants, cab drivers and pets, ever vibrate with sex? Did once those dry Brillo pads that are their cunts ever run with juices? To the victor the spoils. I negotiated my way, sustaining only a minor contusion of the knee from the wheel chair of an ageing Boadicea.

David's penthouse (he never shies from the obvious) was situated at the top (where else?) of a recently constructed apartment block overlooking the trim lawns and much attended flower beds of a railinged square. The garden work is aggressively riotous, and beneath its well-tended and watered turf and soil, for the exclusive use of the occupants of the building, is built discreetly and far from the human eye a multi-storey subterranean car park, where cars are waxed and polished to even more dazzling finish and engines tuned till they purr like lions.

I entered the said building with caution, and why not, for notices warned me that trespassers would be prosecuted and I was nothing but a trespasser, having neither credentials nor suitable attire. The entrance, vulgar to my taste, was marble-lined and floored. Green rubber plants flexed their muscles in a corner pot. At a desk, peak-capped and eagle-eyed, was the porter, who had been watching my approach through the wide glass panoramic doors: trained like a bull mastiff, his eyes focused immediately on the hole in my sock and the red protrusion poking through my sandal which was my September big toe. I shuffled past him, eyes down, heading for the lift.

'Can I help you, sir?' he said, mocking me with that sir. He straightened up to show a pair of shoulders and chest that could crush me in one lazy hug.

'I have an appointment with Mr Adler.'

'I'll let him know you're here, sir. What is your name?'

'Timmins. George Timmins.'

I stood awkwardly in the foyer, a victim of this retired, or axed in all probability, sergeant major, trained killer, his medals boasting his brutishness throughout the four corners of the world. His bluff eyes spelled prejudice at every blink, wop hater, wog beater, hang em, flog em and cut off their bollocks. The full weight of sixty years of cultivated aggression bore down on me as he placed a pencil into the dial of a white telephone and rotated it agonisingly slowly three times. From the lift a man dressed in jodhpurs and riding jacket humped his way down the five carpeted stairs on a pair of stainless steel crutches. Already I was regretting my excursion into the outside world.

In mid dial, the porter replaced the receiver, and hurried to open the door for the no doubt officer war veteran. He escorted the limping major out into the street, standing at a respectful distance, but alert to the task of pulling him to his feet, should the crutches buckle or slide.

I seized my chance and slipped into the lift, pressing the button to the top floor. After a moment's apparent consideration (maybe they too were worked by some mysterious security-conscious electronic eye?) the doors collided like guillotine blades and I hummed my way skywards.

He was dressed in a small silk bathrobe, his legs bare. It was three years since I had seen him last and he looked considerably older. The black hair was beginning to thin at the back and his face looked puffier. His normally dark chin was peppered with stubble. His waist was thicker and there were the beginnings of a paunch. At the top of his cheeks was the slight flush of burst veins, but the eyes above them still had the same sleepy alertness. He smiled. The teeth were dazzlingly white.

'Come in,' he said. I could hear the water running for a bath.

To describe his flat is to describe David, for it is here that the fantasies of his mind are projected as it were onto a living screen. They are inseparable, for David has become this idea, a man who has invented himself rather like one of those collages that were fashionable in the sixties. People made them by cutting out adverts and pictures of pop idols and film stars. He had pieced himself together out of the glittering hardware of consumption and commerce, deliberately, and what is more had lived it out, had seized the 'boom' by the throat, had listened to its extravagant claims with a wry and tuned ear and adopted them as his own. He had set about their acquisition with a clear-headed and practical application; to possess, you needed wealth, and wealth came from a shrewd understanding of how it was made, and of being ahead of those other rivals who were baying for the neon moon. In essence it was simple – you acquired something for considerably less than others were then prepared to pay you for it. An inventive mind and a single-mindedness of purpose open the cave to the magic lamp. It involved effort, treachery, dishonesty, lies, cruelty, flattery, deviousness, but David was nothing but a realist and such demands were not so much the price you had to pay but rather the explicit conditions of play, mere formalities. Morality is in any case merely its practice, and practice, as is well known, makes perfect. Thus he could make his own any of the numerous pieces of gadgetry that our panic-stricken technology is driven to produce. He was like Lot in our modern lottery, ever moving forward, never looking back for fear that the loved one turn to salt – though to be sure in our times someone of enterprise would market her saline remains. But David could acquire and, having acquired, relieve the itch and turn his attention to something else.

Thus although his flat bears testimony in all its extravagant lines to a fantasy, it is already a fantasy that has been laid to rest. His attention is now elsewhere. The flat is more like the remains of the past, a living and centrally heated tomb of Tutankhamun. The walls are lined in a rich gold, and a deep green carpet with a sheen like velvet covers the many-levelled floor. Soft, plump sofas in brown invite the weary visitor to rest. Paintings by some of the best young artists soothe or excite the eye. Lamps occupy corners and tables like preening metal birds, boxes shelter drinks, cases books. The hi-fi envelops you in multitrack sound. Through an arched door the bedroom invites seduction, glittering with wall and ceiling mirrors, reflecting, refracting, in triplicate, quadruplicate, the one solitary six-foot-square bed with its white mink coverlet. Behind its glassy walls, which slide apart at the merest touch of a switch, are lined his suits and jackets, a hundred shirts, a hundred shoes, leather from the hide of alligators, suede from the antelope, silk from the worm, cotton from the loom. The marble bathroom foams with Badedas, and perfumes, green, yellow, rose, propose the elixir of eternal youth.

But for all that, there pervades a mood of disinterest. As I pad my way into the living or 'dying' room I hear the sound of 'Mares eat oats' synthetically syncopating from the colour tv set, which shows the red face of a child. The ash-trays burst with butts, and the glasses that are strewn about the room, some half full, indicate the drinking of the night before. On the sofa *The Times* is scattered and on a low table the remains of his breakfast, a banana and a broken egg shell. Out on the terrace which commands a pano-ramic view of London is an improvised washing line which flaps incongruously with a pair of jockey pants and nylon socks.

He says, 'I'm just going to have a bath. Have a drink.' He scratches his hair and lopes bathwards.

I poured myself a whisky and soda – the first for a long time –ice from the fridge in a heavy glass, and drank. I could see him disrobing through the open door and he got into the water with a contented moan. I read the paper, he soaked and scrubbed and we exchanged remarks that would be of little interest to the reader. It is sufficient to say that some twenty minutes passed before he appeared in a pair of tan trousers, white moccasins and a purple silk shirt. He poured himself a drink and lit a cheroot.

'George, I got trouble,' he said. 'It's nice but it's trouble.' As if to give emphasis to his problems he sank back into the welcoming cushions of the sofa.

Rich, young, powerful and still there are problems! How complex is this life we lead. I raised an eyebrow, indicating a desire to know more.

He exhaled smoke and rubbed his eye, and went on. 'It's a girl. A woman really.'

There had been many women over the years, actresses, models, hairdressers, dress designers, one Olympic hurdles finalist, air hostesses, publishers, theatrical agents, students, a simple heiress or two, and all in their turn had been treated to the overwhelming vitality of his charm, had received telegrams, letters, flowers, gifts, supplications to dine, to dance, to holiday abroad, whatever whim or ruse had entered his head at the time; yet any calculation on his part was only secondary, a sort of inevitable process that ticked over, a knowhow that was always there in half-conscious action, to the genuine feelings that he expressed for them.

For a time at least. In four days of romantic magic, there was nothing that he would not do for his latest paramour. And after an hour of his wit, his attention, his honesty above all, for everyone remarked what an honest person he was about himself and all things, he had, emotionally speaking, bound them hand and foot and there was nothing they would not do for him. Usually his demands were little, and shortly, now inflamed with love for him, the girl would part her inevitably trim and shapely legs on the very white mink spread that covered the six-foot bed next door. In time, usually after some forty-eight hours, the self-induced dream dispelled itself, and he found his Cinderella a thing of rags and tatters on the stroke of midnight and he did not even bother to pick up the glass slippers left behind. If it was slippers he wanted, he could have bought up a whole factory manufacturing them!

But to be fair, he always felt guilty about his sudden change of heart, always blamed himself, fell silent and shifty for almost an hour before he broke the news in an apologetic way. Sometimes so guilty was he that he could not even face the soft bright eyes of his fallen idol, and left the country for a week, for the girl's sake of course, so that she could recover the more easily, free of the tormenting knowledge that he was there in the very same city. But still they came, fresh reinforcements, one after the other, and if you find in my thinking a certain puzzled cynicism with regard to the fairer sex, then I will cite the experience of David Adler by way of explanation. And indeed with the knowledge of all this, it is no wonder that when he spoke to me, I choked a little on the whisky I was drinking and raised the other brow.

He went on, 'I'm mad about her. I can't get enough of her, I want to fuck her every single minute of the day.'

'I'm sorry, I don't understand the problem,' I said, and though I have chosen for myself a different sexual course, or rather a non-sexual course, for I have opted for celibacy after more years of aggravation than I would care at this stage to describe, I am nevertheless puzzled when a fellow human being appears to be enjoying a surfeit of lust.

He looked at me sheepishly, then lowered his eyes, as if deliberating whether he could trust me enough to divulge the burden that lay so heavily on his mind. He hesitated for a moment, then under the pressure of his ill-ease he finally coughed and said with a kind of astonishment, 'But she's really rather ugly.'

Now there is a problem, for if you believe that beauty is, if not truth, then certainly like butter, best, and if you have based most of your thinking life on the predatory acquisition of the best, the fastest car, the loudest hi-fi, the most expensive flat and the most glamorous women, if you worship the appearance and not the essence of things, as most of us do, then indeed the very foundations of that life can creak with insecurity when confronted with a qualitatively different premise. Beauty can reside of course in the eye of the beholder, but usually that same eye looks for reassuring glances of approval from the eyes of others. How could it be otherwise when the major part of the exercise is to compete with and outdo one's neighbour? Beauty is also a thing of fashion, each age producing its own criterion, but for that to operate there must be a generally accepted idea, a concept of loveliness, which the majority will value.

Wherein else resides its worth? (And perhaps David was not formulating it as such, but his eyes and restless mouth reflected it.) Lesser mortals must perforce lower their sights, settle for less, but the dynamic impresarios of our world reach and it is given, take and it is confirmed.

I questioned him and he told me the whole story. I won't attempt to reproduce his hesitations, his pauses, his snatches at cheroots, his repetitions, and indeed his sudden burst of eloquence when a genuine emotion stirred within him at the very mention of her name, but I will take the liberty of a novelist in reducing his account to the more palatable proportions of a chapter, hoping that you will trust my perceptions, my regard for detail and my objectivity.

I merely end on a somewhat carping note: lunch did not seem to be forthcoming, and a good deal of his narrative was punctuated by the cistern-like rumblings of my aroused but frustrated digestive system.

Chapter 4

The story goes like this. Ajax Developments, a subsidiary of the parent company, Adler Enterprises, had turned its ever-eager eye in the direction of Trowbridge Spa to investigate first the possibility of an expansion of holdings and subsequently the development of the city centre. A certain sentimental nostalgia may well have been in the back of the mind of the dynamic thirty-four-year-old tycoon, but he seldom allowed such considerations to influence his shrewd judgements, and it can be safely assumed, though the exact details of the manoeuvre escape my unbusiness-like intelligence, that the investigation must have been founded on a sound commercial basis.

A junior executive of the company first proceeded to that small provincial town, haunted as it is for me by so many childhood memories, made certain discreet enquiries, and returned forthwith with a satisfactory report to his boss. The wheels slowly turning into motion, David himself then ventured forth and got himself invited by the local Rotarians to attend one of their many social functions.

Temperamentally he abhorred such gatherings, but there was the necessity of business dealings. Also the fact that he was returning to his old home town as something of a celebrity, a local boy who had indisputably made good, added an element of flattery to his vanity. For the occasion he had made by his tailor a suit of rich black velvet, which he wore with a cream silk shirt, set off at the neck by a plum red tie. Shoes of the same plum colour were stitched for his feet.

He wanted first to accentuate his distinction, his elegance, before this undoubtedly provincial crowd, but not to the extent of alarming them or making their small-town minds suspicious. He set off in his white Rolls, his chauffeur at the wheel, languidly watching a portable television from the back seat.

They greeted him warmly, laughed at his jokes, were solicitous to his demands. After dinner a speech was given in his honour. All eyes were turned to him. The applause was loud and prolonged.

It was only after dinner, when a five-piece group played from a stage bedecked with carnations, and the Rotarians and their wives or girlfriends danced across a floor slippery with chalk, that he first noticed Maureen. She was dancing with her husband. It was that unquestioned look of boredom in her eyes, as though she had withdrawn her whole personality, that singled her out for him, for that look implied a critical mind and he recognised an ally.

When the music stopped he introduced himself, first to her husband Ted, the owner of a provisions store in the centre of the town, and then to her. He shook her hand and found that it was warm and yielding. When he asked her to dance, Ted grinned with pride at his fellow tradesmen, as his wife took the floor with the distinguished and dashing Mr Adler.

She said, 'I bet you usually don't dance in places like this.' He supposed she was about thirty. She had a certain ripeness, an autumnal quality, like a fruit ready to fall. Her skin was clear, but the flesh pliant. Her hips were heavy with a kind of mysterious sensuality. Next to him she was warm, generating heat, and she moved easily about the floor.

His leg slipped through her parted thighs.

He said with a twinkle, 'It's all in the line of business.'

He had an erection and she nuzzled her soft plump belly into it. When he looked at her face, her eyes flashed back boldly and knowingly. He wanted her immediately.

There was nothing trim, or model-like, or sophisticated about her. She was only too evidently provincial, and it was this perhaps that attracted him. He was now with the kind of woman that if circumstances had been different, if he hadn't been by some accident clever, if he hadn't been to Cambridge, if he hadn't, well practically everything, this was the kind of woman he could have married. It was girls like Maureen that fifteen years before he had kissed on the Common, and, his breath panting with excitement, had moved his eager hand up the abrasive stocking leg, and found, after the initial resistance, clamped knees, wrestling hands, the delicious damp slippery prize. He remembered seducing his first girl on his parents' bed, surrounded by their three-piece suite, the mirror of the dressing table with its cut-glass dishes and trays, purely ornamental, never used, reflecting his own satanic face in its reproachful oval surface; beneath him the disorderly stockinged legs of the girl, her damp knickers round her ankles, her shoulders heaving on the green sateen bedspread. Oh, that bedspread evoked in him such vibrant lust! For hours he had rubbed and rubbed with soap and water and cloth the large dark stain that his semen left, and for all his scrubbing it remained, desecrating the prim sanctity of his mother's sleep. All this, with its hints of guilt and secrecy and desire, Maureen released in him, and he wanted her all the more.

All evening he danced with her and when the group thumped out the last waltz amid the wilting flowers, he said to her, 'I must see you again. Do you ever come up to London?' She said simply, 'For you I would.'

So he escorted her back to her table and back to her husband, and thanked them all for a most enjoyable evening, and when he shook Ted's hand, he offered him his card, saying, 'Any time you're in London,' and left for his car.

For a week he waited, restless, aroused, laughing at himself for his absurdity, but when the telephone rang and she said,

'I'm at Charing Cross station,' all self-reproach vanished and he waited impatiently for her to arrive.

She wore a belted suede coat and underneath a short angora dress in ice blue. She had white knee-length boots. She smiled at him self-consciously but mischievously at the door, like someone in the wrong. He took her coat and her perfume caught his nostrils. It had been a long time since he smelled that heady cologne.

She sat down while he poured her a drink. He could see from her face the awe and excitement that his flat made her feel, for her eyes darted here and there, taking in that painting, that colour, that object, but always they returned to him with a kind of nervous expectancy.

He found himself curiously tongue-tied. Once in her presence he could think of nothing to say. He wanted to hold her, that was all. Already he was aroused in the same way as before. It was marvellous, so urgent a sensation.

She said, 'Well, I came,' and sipped her drink, looking at him over the rim.

He sat next to her. 'I can't think of anything to say,' he said. 'Except I want you.'

She gave a nervous laugh, then put her arms round his neck and kissed him. It was a rushing, breathless, eager, impulsive desire that he felt. He hugged her close to him and she wriggled and he held her even tighter.

He made love to her there on the sofa, her angora dress around her bum and her tights at her ankles.

Afterwards he lay on her belly and she stroked his hair. She said, 'I knew it would be like that.'

He made her tea, it was what she wanted, and laughingly he thought how right it was. While he brewed in the kitchen she wandered about the room, looking at this, picking up that. It was curious that the delight she took in his possessions was so akin to his, or what it had been before he grew bored with them. Her very simple pleasure recharged those forgotten relics with a new kind of meaning. He saw them through her eyes and revalued them. She wanted to know where he had bought them, why, how much he had paid. He was offhand in his replies and that made her marvel all the more.

When they finished tea, he picked her up in his arms, she protesting how heavy she was and he agreeing, and carried her to the bedroom. He took off her clothes slowly this time, savouring her, but he made love to her with as much intensity and as much joy.

He lay back astounded. It had never been like this before, so free of anxiety and manipulation and cunning. He had merely followed his impulses, and his impulses did the rest. It was so easy.

He turned to her and saw that she was sobbing, silently at first, but when he asked what was wrong, it was as if by admitting her tears he had conferred upon her a freedom, and she sobbed uncontrollably, great heaving gasps from the depths of her, hailstones of tears welling in her eyes, and flooding the mascara onto her cheeks. He squeezed her hand and she stammered, 'I'm sorry,' but the sobs still came, and when finally they seemed to abate and her breathing became more regular he asked tenderly, 'What's the matter?' And she shook her head as if it was all beyond her comprehension.

He gave her a cigarette and she smiled and lit up. Then she gave a short laugh and said, 'I don't suppose you want to see me again.'

And he shook his head as if in amazement and said, 'Oh yes, I do.'

'Really?' she said, her eyebrows in a curve.

'Really,' he said.

And he did, the next Thursday, and the next and the next, in fact every Thursday for the following three months.

Which brings us up to date and me sitting in his penthouse flat, hungry but silently impressed by his story. And he too was moved by it, for when he had finished he sat for a long time without saying anything, pulling occasionally at the top of his left sock. Finally he said, 'I don't suppose you remember her. She was at the same junior school. Lower down. Maureen White used to be her name.'

But I had to shake my head, for the name escaped me. Indeed it is curious but I remember almost no girls at that school, except the one who sat behind me, who would whisper to me occasionally to look under the desk where she would show me her small, pink, infant-like vagina. And even then I can place no name to the memory.

'I'd like you to meet her though. She's coming here this afternoon. OK?'

And what could I do, but nod my head and grin and say, 'OK.'

Chapter 5

She was due to arrive at three o'clock, and by two-thirty he was in a noticeable state of agitation. He kept pacing back from the terrace to the main room, glancing at his watch and mumbling to himself. And his anxiety could not have been reduced much by the sound of the vacuum cleaner, which a stout and disapproving housekeeper was humping around the flat. She made a great deal of the full ashtrays and unwashed glasses, clattering them to show her hostility. And I must admit that I was not without a certain sympathy for her, even though she made it quite clear that she considered me to be one of the enemy camp. She hunted me from chair to chair, wherever I fled to escape her infernal machine.

With such a noise conversation was impossible, but even had we been in the most silent of soundproofed rooms, I had the feeling that he would not have spoken or paid any attention to me whatsoever. He had said his piece and was now anxious to get on with the next business, whatever that was to be, and somehow for all my thoughts on the subject, I could not for the life of me see how it could include me. I joined him on the terrace where he was leaning over a balustrade, flicking matches over the side and watching them float to the street below. I suspect he was timing the fall with his watch.

'Perhaps I ought to go,' I said.

His reply was short and rather irritable. 'No, you stay. Have a drink or get yourself something to eat from the fridge. Mrs Lot'll cook you something when she's finished.' He placed another match between finger and thumb and fired it streetwards.

'But why do you want me to stay?' I insisted.

He leaned both elbows onto the balustrade and stared down.

'I want your opinion. You know something about women and psychiatry. Jesus!' he exclaimed. The last being prompted by the sight of a taxi cab that as it were in slow motion had steered itself maniacally into the side of a Morris Minor in the street below. There was the usual squeal of brakes and that awful hollow crashing sound of impact, rather like a sack of scrap iron dropped onto an empty steel drum. The head of the driver of the Morris was poking bloodily through the windscreen and I moved away, unable to watch any longer.

I returned to the living room, which was now silent and orderly. Mrs Lot washed dishes in the kitchen. If anything, his enigmatic answer to my question had succeeded in confounding me all the more. What on earth did he mean by 'You know something about women and psychiatry?' I racked my brains to find some clue to the origins of this strange assumption.

It is true that I had undergone a somewhat abbreviated form of psychoanalysis. For two years, three times a week, for fifty-minute sessions, I had lain on a couch rambling on about my life and my dreams, waiting for the mysterious 'transference' to take place, and whether it did or not to this day I am uncertain. I retain the greatest respect for my analyst, who seemed a patient if mainly silent man and endured with gravity the boredom of my life and the occasional scandals, but whether his insights or mine finally gave me 'freedom of choice' is debatable both in a personal sense and, even more so, in a philosophical one. I will say that the chronic anxiety states that gripped me, the floodings, the sleeplessness, the palpitations of the heart, the sweating palms and the fear of death did abate somewhat.

And I suppose that this was not entirely coincidental, but after two years I arrived at the conclusion that possibly it was less expensive, more beneficial and certainly less solipsistic to confront the reality of the objective world such as I understood it, rather than rely upon the somewhat narrow confines of the thrice-weekly sessions as the central axis of my experience. In analysis all roads seem to lead to the couch. However, taking my fragile psyche into my hands, I terminated the treatment with hardly any protests from the mild voice that had made occasional pronouncements literally behind my back. We shook hands finally and at length tentatively looked into each other's eyes and smiled. His face bore all the marks of the most terrible depressions and I suspect he had somewhat less faith in the analytic process than I had. In any case, I think he gave the practice up and the last I heard of him, he was living in a sleeping bag in the depths of Epping Forest, finding therapy in a rather less scientific way in communion with nature.

As to a knowledge of women, I can speak only with the rather plaintive and exhausted voice of failure. Most of my earlier experiences with the opposite sex were based, or so it seemed to me, on the most elementary of misunderstandings. In their minds my sole raison d'être, so to speak, was to answer their every whim and uncertainty, whereas I on the other hand wanted nothing so much as to be left contentedly alone with my own preoccupations. What I never understood is how I always seemed to single out the same kind of girl. Put me in a room full of women and, to be sure, drawn by some magnetic process in the ether, madam would seek me out, the kind who wanted Jesus Christ and Mephistopheles rolled into one, who wanted the world's knowledge placed at her disposal in one palatable ball that could be assimilated without effort or curiosity, who wanted advice and insight into what was to be her eventual role in life, and who saw every independent action on my part as a threat to her own security.

From this I can deduce that all women are exactly the same, or behave in exactly the same way with me. Or else for whatever inner motives, and I suspect it was really little more than fatigue, I colluded with that particular archetype.

Needless to say, all these qualities were honed to perfection in the woman I chose to marry. Madeline had a deep-rooted conviction that my one ambition in life was to destroy her. I could do this by reading a book, not speaking at breakfast, shaving, conversing with friends, or lecturing at schools to keep her in the style to which she was unaccustomed. She retaliated in myriad aggressive ways too numerous and, for me, painful to recount, but I will say by way of a hint that it is remarkable how much hostility can go into the frying of an egg. It lasted five years and in that time she bore me two sons, who then, I regret to say, and if you will forgive the pun, bored me. They were noisy and artful and refined blackmail into an art form. Needless to say, Madeline used them as weapons against me. I remember once when Toby was four: he had taken to blowing down a piece of bent gas pipe, producing a sound not dissimilar to a bugle. In one of my sporadic efforts to simulate the interest of a father, I said, 'Do you want to play the trumpet when you grow up?' He looked me straight in the eye and said without a trace of even juvenile irony, 'I want to do everything.' Frankly, I found his Oedipus complex tiresome. For all I cared, he could have his mother, lock, stock and barrel.

It was little erosions like this that prompted me finally into some form of action. Academia I couldn't stand, its enclosed and vicious pretentiousness, the anxiety states that shook me nightly and that Madeline in her wisdom would cite as only further proof of my lack of devotion to her.

And then one morning I woke up early with the kind of throbbing erection that I hadn't experienced for years, and it was with some sense of horror that I realised that I would like to direct it between the thighs of almost any woman in the world other than the one beside me. I packed my bags and left, gave up my lectureship, took a room and lived on the dole, which I have been doing for the last five years.

One pays of course for these decisions. I was paralysed from the waist down for two months, but in that time I thought a lot and reaffirmed my decision. And Madeline, once free of my enslaving influence, or so she told the world, began to edit a small literary journal, which relieved me of the financial burden of supporting her. As an arrangement it works quite well. I have few needs and few complaints. I leave women alone and satisfy my sexual requirements with my own friendly right hand.

So you will appreciate somewhat my surprise at David's response. I suppose it did occur to me that he perhaps saw in my retreat from the world a certain mystical significance which the worldly do often attribute to the poor. Perhaps in renouncing Oxford and Madeline, I had aspired to a higher state of consciousness and wisdom in my part-furnished Paddington room, and could proffer guidance from my guru-like heights. But as I looked at him standing out there on the terrace, the wind ruffling his thinning hair, looking out at the skyline of London, part of which he owned, it occurred to me that perhaps there was no one else in this world that he could come to for advice.

At ten minutes to three Mrs Lot stacked away the last saucepan and said, 'Will that be all Mr Adler?' Her tone implied murder would be committed if there were further instructions.

He shook his head. 'Thank you very much, Mrs Lot.'

'I'll do the shirts tomorrow,' she said and was gone.

His reaction to her departure was sudden, and to me unexpected. He rushed down from the terrace and closed the door after her, in a way that suggested he had been impatient with her presence for some time. He looked at me almost desperately and spoke hurriedly.

'I'm sorry about that, but it was impossible to talk with her here. She listens to everything. And in my position I never know whether she's being paid by someone else to spy.'

I looked at him disbelievingly, for I associated this kind of paranoia only with episodes in television serials, but one look at his face which was tense and quite without humour confirmed his conviction. I suddenly had a new insight into the intricacies of a life that depends as much on secrecy and double dealing as a secret agent's. He was in a fiercely competitive business.

'Well, why don't you sack her?' I said, helpfully I thought.

He brushed this aside. Other matters were now his concern.

'Look, Maureen's been complaining that I never take her

47

out, that I never introduce her to any of my friends. She's suddenly got rather touchy about it. You know what women are like. I told her I'd introduce you to her.'

It had all been arranged in his mind beforehand. I could not but help feel resentful that he had been so certain of my complicity. A sadder reflection made me think that perhaps he had no friends.

'But why me?'

'For Christ's sake, who else can I introduce her to?'

It was the kind of remark, ambiguous enough, and characteristic of him, to make interpretation a thing of infinite possibility. On the one hand, it could mean that I was the only person to whom he could entrust such a prize, and on the other, and I suspect that this was much nearer the truth, that Maureen was not considered fit to move in the circles that he had access to, and that I was the only person he knew who would not compromise him.

I began to feel more than a little sympathy for the unfortunate girl's misgivings, and resentful at the way that he was prepared to exploit our past association, I resisted.

'I don't think that's very fair.'

He looked at me intently with those soft grey-green eyes. His voice had a velvet edge. 'George, I'm just asking you to do me a favour, that's all. I need your help.' It sounded so simple, a cry from the heart, ringing with sincerity, forged out of need, but with David, consummate actor that he was, it was impossible to distinguish the line between falsehood and truth, and I believe that he had precisely the same difficulty. At best you took him on trust, with the caution of a tradesman, hoping his credit was good and the cheque would not bounce. It says something for his personality that usually you took the risk, and I capitulated by saying, 'What do you want me to do?'

His mood changed instantly. He was now eager and forceful.

'She's a small town girl and she has all the illusions of the bright lights. Rich, exciting, trendy London. It would really give her a buzz to talk to you. Tell her you're a writer. That's all. Make her feel she's with the big time.'

He could see from my face that he was losing my support. 'Look, it's no skin off your nose, is it? Just for half an hour?' He looked again at his watch. She would be arriving at any moment.

By now I suspect I wanted to see her almost as much as he did, for there was something curious about this affair and I wanted to discover more about it, if only to check his account against my own impressions. It certainly offered something more interesting than I could find in my own flat at three o'clock on a Thursday afternoon. I wondered, irrelevantly, if the mouse was still there.

'OK,' I said.

'Well then for Christ's sake go into my bedroom and put some clothes on, so that you at least look the part. And hurry up.'

The element of charades did not escape me, but once committed I began to enjoy the new role that had been allotted to me. I flicked carefully and thoughtfully through the row of trousers, with one eye certainly on the future. A dark brown corduroy trouser took my fancy, somewhat loose around the waist but a supple rhinoceros belt with a brass buckle took in the surplus inches. I chose a bright yellow cotton shirt and an antelope suede jacket. A soft pair of light fawn calf-length boots hid the holes in my socks. I wrapped my old clothes into a neat bundle and pushed them under the bed. A sprinkle of Prince Gourielli aftershave gave an odorous touch to the transformation. Glancing into the all-enveloping mirrors, I was not altogether displeased with my appearance. I sauntered into the living room, the epitome of success.

'Feel free,' he said, somewhat grudgingly I thought, and it crossed my mind that in my newly elevated state I might offer him some form of not inconsiderable competition. I think he was wary of this too, but before it could develop further, perhaps resulting in a change of plans on his part, the door bell rang, and the lady, of whom I had, in such a relatively short space of time, heard so much, entered the room.

Chapter 6

I had imagined someone quite different of course. The picture I had been building up in my mind was, unaccountably, blonde, blue-eyed, short, timid and plump. Maureen was none of these things. Her hair was dark and cut short with a fringe that topped a high forehead, black brows and brown mischievous eyes, almond-shaped, which gave her a slightly oriental look. The nose was uneven and sharp, and perhaps it was this feature that threw out the balance of her face, or maybe the chin was also too uncompromisingly defined to accommodate to more conventional lines of beauty. One felt in a strange way that her face was a near miss: a slight adjustment here, a fraction off there, and she would have been a woman of stunning looks, but nature had dealt otherwise and produced something merely coarse. Her complexion was clear and ruddy.

But it was her body that drew the attention. She was tall, five foot eight perhaps, with the most wonderfully long and supple legs, and her belly and thighs were a masterpiece of succulence and sensuality, swelling voluptuously beneath her dress. It is a shape not currently in fashion, but a shape that is full of hints and suggestions. In a word, there was something of the showgirl in her. Yet her manner, which was petulant and girlish, seemed totally at odds with her body, as though she seemed unaware of her attraction, or if she did was somehow dissociating herself from it. It is a characteristic of many English women who are seldom really at home in their bodies.

David opened the door for her, and I could see her smile at him. She put her arms round his waist and kissed him. She was wearing a scarlet beret. She noticed me across his shoulder and she gave me a nervous embarrassed laugh, biting her lower lip apologetically.

'I'm dreadfully sorry,' she said. 'I didn't know anyone was here. I don't know what you must think of me.' She had that flat London accent that is common from Southwark to the south coast. When she was nervous and uncertain, as she was now in my presence, she tried to sound 'refined'.

He took her hand and led her across the room. 'It's all right, it's George.'

She opened her mouth in a kind of gasp of recognition and relief. 'Oh I've heard so much about you. I'm very pleased to meet you.' She extended her hand.

I wondered exactly what it was that he had told her, and I began to feel slightly as one does in those dreams when for no apparent reason one is thrust onto a stage in a leading part knowing neither the character nor the lines, and I looked across at him for some clue, but his face gave none. He contented himself merely with smiling at her in the way that an indulgent father might smile at his eldest daughter. I shook her hand and nodded my pleasure.

She sat on the sofa, first smoothing her skirt, her long legs crossed in front of her and her hands clasped around her knee. She looked first at him and then at me, smiling as if to fill the silence that had suddenly descended. He sat beside her.

'Did you have any problems getting here?'

She shook her head, 'I got a taxi straight from the station.' Then she laughed. 'You'd have rolled up on the train. It was jam-packed, my compartment, and there was this drunk in the corner. Singing to himself. And you know how people won't open their mouths on trains. They were all reading the papers ignoring him. I was pretending to do the crossword. I've no idea how you do them, but I just fill in any old word, so people'll think I'm intellectual!' At this she screwed up her face and made a tutting sound of self-deprecation. 'Anyway the train stopped and it must have been his station. You know, the drunk. Well he got up and opened the door on the wrong side. It was like a four-foot drop. And he was just about to step out, and everyone knew and no one said a word. So I tapped him on the shoulder and I said, "Excuse me," I said, "you want the other side." So he muttered something and staggered over to the other door and got out. And then the man in the corner right by the door had the cheek to lift his head and say, "Drunk, I suppose," then he went bright red and went back to his paper. I nearly died.'

It was home, it was everything we had ever grown up with, and what was more it was something we had lost. Her delivery was fast, self-mocking and shrewd at the same time. It was a stance to life formed out of suspicion and caution, expecting nothing but what you could extract from the ingredients. I agree there is more than an element of sentimentality in my assessment, a tendency perhaps to romanticise, but in the curiously artificial and contrived atmosphere of that penthouse, with its expensive fittings and self-conscious fixtures, it was the breath of life itself. It brought us together and made us relax.

We spent a pleasant half hour, reminiscing about our childhood, about our school, about the places we knew. 'I think it's wonderful that you two have stayed friends for so long,' she said. Then out of the blue, her eyes shining with curiosity, she added, 'David says you write films.'

It was a shock. It reminded me immediately of the somewhat unpleasant task that I was there to fulfil, yet I had not been prepared for this particular role. Again I looked at David for assistance, but he merely returned my glance with all the insolence of one who is preparing to enjoy as spectator the game that is about to begin. Throughout the whole conversation they had sat hand in hand.

I stroked my chin and said, 'Sometimes,' hoping that

perhaps my diffidence would close the matter there, but far from it.

'It must be wonderful being in films,' she said. 'I suppose you know all the people. What are they like?'

'Just like any one else really.'

'Oh, come on,' she reproached me. 'You probably think I'm stupid and all that, but I'd love to know all the gossip. I mean do you know Michael Caine?'

Falsehood is an activity like any other; to excel at it a commitment is necessary, and committed, albeit against my will, I had to be. I spoke of adultery, of affairs or personal secrets, of tricks of the trade, of perversions, of swimming pools, the whole boring catalogue that is the stock in trade of those other liars who work in publicity.

She listened with a ferocious attention, interpolating from time to time exclamations such as 'No!' or 'I don't believe it' or 'Never!' while she squeezed David's hand and looked for confirmation in his collusive eyes.

I will admit here that part of the inspiration of my performance, and seen in a purely objective light it must be judged a minor tour de force, was revenge. I took on the role of raconteur and man about town in the not particularly commendable hope that by thus establishing myself I would somewhat diminish David's allure in her eyes. I had no other motive in this than revenge for the offensive position he had placed me in. But if that is what I set out to do I had badly misjudged the lady. Rather than eclipse his sun, I added only to his lustre. It was as if my own prowess merely reflected back his glory. She loved him all the more, while I felt jester to his eminence. Throughout he smiled benignly on us both.

But like all entertainers jesters have their entrances and their exits and I could see from the way he began looking at his watch that the time for my departure was approaching. In this respect he could never forget the acquired manner of the boardroom, where schedules were schedules and audiences were duly given in line with the maxim 'time is money'. He got up abruptly from the sofa and stood waiting for me to take my leave.

In answer to my cue, I stood rubbing my hands. 'Well, I'd better be off.'

'Oh, must you?' She looked disappointed but this was only an unconvincing mask, for her eyes told otherwise. She was already impatient for him and he for her, and so I left them with their desire and perhaps more than a little envy.

At least, I thought as I descended the lift, girding myself to meet the assault of the porter, at least I've acquired a new outfit.

Chapter 7

The events of that day disturbed me, and not simply in the way you might expect of an impoverished recluse, perhaps dropout. In fact, my whole psychic metabolism had been shaken up. Not the least of my difficulties would be to explain to the Ministry of Employment and Productivity, or the horn of plenty as it is known locally, why it was that I was now sporting brown corduroy trousers, a yellow shirt, suede jacket and calf-length boots, for my entire wardrobe had for some time been limited to that shabby bundle lying under David Adler's six-foot bed, and if I judged Mrs Lot's character accurately, its stay there would be of a limited nature. Within twenty-four hours, I was convinced, it would be consigned to the incinerator or to whatever other means the rich use to dispose of their refuse.

But what dominated my thoughts was the pair that I had left together in the penthouse, or to be more precise one of that pair, namely Maureen. David's motives and fantasies seemed to me at any rate at that stage reasonably clear, but I felt I knew so little about that tall girl who had cheered me so and to whom I had given so false a display. About the last I felt guilty, for the deception had shown contempt for her, the contempt that every trickster and faker and secondhand car dealer has for his dupe. It was so unlike me, I felt, but then what is 'like' and 'unlike'? As a rule the circumstance dictates. We hope that past experience guides our actions, or the rationalists do; the godly are under the illusion that the almighty has a hand, and the 'scientific' blame their amoral genes. But to my thinking, what I do is invariably a belated response to an outside world that continues perversely and independently of my wishes.

Quite simply, I wanted to know who Maureen was, where she came from, and what she did. I was restless with curiosity and, if I have been doing my job correctly, and God knows it's a difficult and thankless task, and if at this point in the narrative I still have a few hardy readers left, they will likewise, I hope, be sharing this curiosity. In the real course of events I had to wait some time before I could assemble sufficient information for a reliable biography, but it would merely be perverse of me to withhold it at this stage, so without further ado I will set your minds at rest.

Maureen was thirty, married and childless. She was the only child of a working-class family in Trowbridge Spa, her father being a quiet, obviously depressed man, who felt ill at ease with the world in general and with his wife and daughter in particular. He felt himself always an outsider, paralysed by an inability to communicate; the simplest request filled him with anxiety. Some terrible nameless despair seemed to hold him in its grip. It was there strapped across his back when he woke in the morning, and he took it with him to work and brought it home at night. It made him a quiet methodical worker, a bricklayer by trade, dependable, not disliked by his workmates, but then on the other hand not really noticed. At tea breaks he drank his mug and ate his sandwiches, listening to the stories the other men told, seldom telling any in return. He worked hard and conscientiously, anxious only to provide for his wife and later his daughter.

When she was born, he was filled with the most terrible misgivings, for war had just broken out, and he saw in it an ominous warning to him. He wondered whether he had the right to bring a child into this kind of world. When he looked into the cradle she seemed so small and helpless, so fragile that even one careless touch from his rough, cement-burnt hands might break her in two. From that moment he felt somehow unworthy of her.

And this feeling was more than encouraged by his wife, a small dark rodent of a woman with eyes that were always frantically scanning horizons. It remains a mystery why she ever married him, for she thought him coarse and slow-witted and 'common'. She herself had other aspirations, not so much for herself but for her daughter, though she dressed as well as his money would allow and preened herself on Sundays at the local Congregational Church where she was much renowned for her singing voice and admired for her renderings at concert parties of light musical comedy numbers, gatherings which her husband (much to his credit) solidly and unshakeably refused to attend. From the start she dressed Maureen in silks and satins and little white boots and when her hair was long enough she curled it into long dark ringlets with hot tongs. She fussed over her and petted her and protected her from the coarse childish pursuits of the street. When Maureen was old enough for school, mother took daughter's hand and led her there, wept slightly as she disappeared in her tartan kilt and matching tam-o'-shanter into the alien care of a teacher. She was there again at the gate when the bell went and it was time to go home. Maureen often wondered whether her mother merely waited outside in all weathers, never going home.

But all this attention was merely a preamble, a preparation for the big goal. When she was six Maureen was enrolled at the MacGregor School of Dancing, Ballet and Tap. It involved considerable expense, but Gladys White was not one to be thwarted by such vulgar considerations when her daughter's whole future was at stake. In her mind she could see her young offspring moving with all the grace that deportment lessons can bring through the salons of the rich and famous, she could see her making her debut in the West End of London, the star of an extravagant new musical or even the prima ballerina at Sadlers Wells. Was this opportunity to be thrown aside for the sake of a few pounds? Gladys thought not and it is to her credit that she sacrificed so much with such little thought for herself. She took a part-time job as a sales lady in a local department store.

In this world, alas, sacrifice is no guarantee of talent and it has to be admitted that Maureen, despite all the opportunities, did not show exceptional flare as a dancer. She skipped about with the other young ladies of her age while Miss MacGregor struck out chords on a much abused Bechstein, she moved her little feet encased in blocked shoes from first position to fifth, she held her young arms above her head and did arabesques and jetés, she passed her various grades, but only a doting mother could fail to see that she would never make a ballerina.

She had more aptitude for tap, As she grew older and her legs longer, she did several cute little numbers which involved high kicks and ended with the splits. She appeared in many shows and always aroused a certain attention at the annual gala performance that the school gave in the Town Hall. At every show, Gladys was there, fussing around her daughter, combing her hair, giving her little presents, consoling, encouraging, and admiring from the front row of the stalls. By her side sat her husband, poor Tom White, in his Sunday best, watching the Dance of the Rosebuds or the routine accompanying the Desert Song, feeling apprehension for his daughter in his silent way, trying his hardest to hide the embarrassment that he could not but feel for the heavy feet and shrill voices of the juvenile troupe.

But it would seem his apprehension was misplaced, for Maureen loved her dancing. She lived for it, every single moment of it. She showed not the slightest resentment towards her fussing mother, and it was only her father with his silent brooding presence and rough hands who frightened her. She echoed all her mother's contempt for him, and whenever he tried to chastise her, she tossed her black ringlets and flounced away. She took as her own all her mother's hopes and aspirations. She was convinced that things would turn out as her mother had planned. They always had, so why should it be otherwise?

The pattern is clear. For Maureen, her mother was comforter, guide, arbiter of taste, fate and fortune rolled into one. Imagine therefore the total loss, as if the world itself had lost its axis, when this compulsive and domineering woman suffered a sudden seizure on a warm evening in July and died three days later of a fatal heart attack in the local hospital. Maureen was fourteen years old at the time.

The death overwhelmed her. It was so sudden, so inexplicable and so absolutely irrevocable. She felt completely alone, abandoned, like the half-finished peasant costume her mother had been making for the next show when her heart so cruelly gave up. The dress lay on the floor where it had fallen that fateful evening, a terrible reminder of Maureen's incompleteness. After the funeral she gathered it up in her arms and sobbed her wretched grief into it. She locked herself in her room and refused to eat or speak to her silent bewildered father for three days, and when she finally emerged, her eyes puffy, red, but now dry, it was with a defeated recognition that life could never be the same again.

The atmosphere in the house between father and daughter became unbearably tense. Poor Tom White could see in his wife's death yet another reprimand from the vengeful gods for his own terrible unspoken crimes as though he were responsible for it in some devious way, and he retreated further into himself and remained almost constantly silent. They sat together at their evening meal, which Maureen now prepared, not speaking one word, the silence broken only by the clink of knife and fork, or the sounds of their teeth chewing her inexpertly cooked food.

Afterwards Tom turned on the television and stared bleakly at it till his eyes blurred into sleep.

To lose her mother was one thing but to be left alone with this ignorant stupid brute was more than she could bear, and her whole life and thinking became directed towards the one preoccupation of getting away.

But where to? Like thousands of others, she left school at fifteen with an education that qualified her for practically nothing. She could type accurately but slowly, her spelling was erratic, she could dance of course, but the junior employment officer who came to the school knew of no vacancies for dancers and recommended her for the typing pool in the accounts department of the regional office of the Mutual Insurance Company.

At first there was a certain kind of excitement, new faces, office gossip, the sense of being adult, of earning a living, but after a few short months the meagre wage packet at the end of the week seemed little compensation for the actual physical drudgery and boredom of the work. And it became clear to her that rather than offer an escape route for her, the office was yet another obstacle, along with her home and father, that she had to escape from. She sat in the pool, the incessant noise of typewriters chattering in her ear, dreaming of sunshine and faraway places, theatres where she was the star, and rich young men who drove up in their sports cars and said, 'Let me take you away from all this.'

It would be easy to ask why Maureen didn't do as others had. If she wanted to be a dancer why didn't she go to London, for example, for an audition, why didn't she write letters to agents, why didn't she read the appropriate journal? To such people I can only say that they have no idea of life in the provinces. Maureen did none of these things in the first place because she had no idea that this was the procedure and knew no one who could advise her. And second, the gulf that appears to separate small town life from the 'glamour' of show business is perceived as so vast, so distant as to be wholly unbridgeable. The reality of the sheer drudgery of the life of most professional chorus dancers, which certainly was all that Maureen could ever hope to aspire to, is another matter, and very far from the fantasies that sustained her at her desk, but even this kind of work, and here I do not mean to be patronising, seemed as unreachable as the peak of Everest or the moon. Maureen had her dreams, and dreams they remained and that was all. If the secretly hoped-for 'talent scout', who would see her one day at the Town Hall and whisk her off to be a star, figured very large in Maureen's imaginings, it was nothing more than a palliative to the boredom of her everyday existence.

Maureen was restless, full of yearnings and hopes and daydreams, but she was stuck there in the typing pool, and as her adolescence matured into early womanhood she began to realise that she must find some other way out, and her thoughts turned to marriage.

She had several boyfriends and was not unpopular. Her dancing gave her a certain notoriety in the town and sons of local tradesmen took her to the cinema, furtively placing an arm round her shoulder and leaving it there, rigid with cramp, until the closing credits of the film. They took her for drives in their fathers' cars out into the country where they parked and kissed her, and breathed heavily, and slid their hands into her bra and tickled her nipples and sometimes, emboldened, groped up her skirt for her knickers. She almost always drew the line here and kept her legs firmly shut, whereupon they apologised and drove her home, and then tried it again the next time. Occasionally she succumbed, for it was not unpleasant and she discovered that an occasional favour bestowed paid dividends in popularity. By the time she was nineteen she had never, as she told her girlfriends, 'gone all the way'.

It was about then that she met Ted Hardin, the only son of parents who kept a small grocery store in the centre of the town. He had just been demobilised from two years' National Service in the RAF and he seemed consequently to Maureen very mature and experienced. Furthermore he had been stationed in Singapore and Maureen thrilled to his descriptions of the Orient, of sunny beaches, of wild neon-lit night life. He told her how cheap things were there, how watches, cameras, radios could be bought for a song. She was especially impressed that a native tailor had made him shirts for the price of a hundred cigarettes.

Ted, the warrior, had returned from defending his native country's interests in the Far East, full of ambition and determination. The business had now been handed over to him, or rather he was buying it from his parents in modest weekly instalments. He had plans and such plans! He aimed to transform the small shop, with its marble counters, its old-fashioned bacon slicer and antiquated scales, its fresh eggs and made-up butter, its Lipton's teas and liver sausage, into Trowbridge Spa's first supermarket.

To assist him in this Napoleonic empire-building task, he needed the love and companionship of a good woman, and for his money, modest though it was at that stage, he could do no better than Maureen. He booked a table for two at Warly Manor Country Club, dinner and dance thirty bob a head, and after soup, roast duck and crème caramel, washed down with Beaujolais Villages, he proposed.

She was rather taken aback and asked if she could think about it. He said he understood and would wait. She started to think there and then and continued to do so in the car home. Twenty-four hours later she made up her mind. He was not unattractive, was ambitious, was well thought of about the town, and would make a go of the business. He had mentioned that they would live in the flat above the shop, which was not entirely to her taste, but would do as a start. She telephoned him the next day from a call box and said her answer was yes.

He was beside himself with joy and immediately began preparations for the big day. It was understood and agreed by his parents that given the special circumstances of Maureen's background and her father being only a bricklayer, they would overlook normal etiquette and would foot the bill for the reception themselves. It was to be a church wedding and came the day Maureen processed on her dancer's legs down the aisle, clad in shimmering satin with a peekaboo bow in her hair, and stood beside the topped and tailed figure of her husband to be. The church was packed with the groom's relatives all in their best, a carnation in each lapel. In view of the special circumstances of Maureen's background, Tom White was not invited to participate. In fact she never saw her father after that and it seems he took to drink, of which he died some years later.

They honeymooned in London at the Strand Palace Hotel – it was Maureen's idea – and in a week she packed in as many shows and films as she could. She felt, sitting in the deep backs of taxis, wearing a new outfit, and the bright avenues of the city gliding past, that perhaps her dream was beginning.

But the honeymoon over, she found herself behind the counter of the shop. Ted said, 'I don't really like the idea of you working, but for the time being it'll help to get us on our feet.' And in truth for the time being Maureen didn't mind too much. It gave her a sense of proprietorship, of position, nodding to the customers, taking their orders and their money, placing it in the till, watching it mount up. In the evening when Ted did the day's take, the figures themselves seemed to promise a whole bright new future, and when she paid it into the bank next day there was the security that it was safe, growing and hers. The typing pool seemed a long way away.

For a year she worked happily enough. At weekends they drove to the country or the seaside and Ted was always generous with little presents, surprises, treats. They attended functions, dinner dances. They made a striking pair. It is difficult to pinpoint any one thing that made her feel suddenly restless – it was probably an accumulation of things – but the turning point came when she noticed her hands, how red they were getting. She looked at them in horror and had a sudden fear that they would grow as red as the hams she sliced. She became aware of the smells of the shop, of the meat, of the cardboard boxes in the damp cellar, the cheeses that stank of feet. The coins that she took seemed to soil her, with their dark and grimy copper and nickel. And there seemed no escape from it. The flat above the shop, on which she had lavished such attention in the first few months of their marriage, which she had filled with such bright colours, oranges and greens and check, seemed contaminated by the smells below. Even her bedroom with its soft net curtains and white bedspread seemed defiled by it all. She took baths obsessively as if she could soak and scrub the odour out, for she was sure everything, her clothes, her body, reeked of groceries. She lavished perfume on her body, lotion on her hands, but whatever she did the smell still seemed to be there.

She burst into tears one night, crying uncontrollably. 'I can't stand it any more. It's not right. I shouldn't have to work in the shop. I'm not a skivvy. Ted,' she said, grasping him suddenly by the shoulders, looking into his surprised face, 'we must buy a house, somewhere away from the shop. A new bungalow out near the country. Please, Ted, I can't stand it here. How can I be pretty for you, working in all that meat and cheese?'

Ted saw her distress and pondered over it. He spent almost the entire night working over the accounts, seeing how much a new assistant would add to the budget and eat into profits, assessing the cost of a mortgage. He came to the conclusion that if he took on a young trainee her wage would not be exorbitant, and if they let the flat above the shop, the acquired rent would meet their mortgage repayments. It was all very feasible and he told her in the morning that she could stop work and they could begin looking for the bungalow of their dreams.

She found one on a new estate five miles outside town. It had a large lounge with big picture windows, a small dining room with a hatch through from the kitchen, a medium-sized bedroom and small spare room, and a modern bathroom with basin, bath and WC all in matching pink. It was centrally heated throughout. The garden was a mass of rubble and old cement bags that the builders had left, but she could see in time how it could be transformed with a green lawn and neat, colourful flower beds. She made up her mind on sight and Ted was happy that she was happy. It was a bargain at two thousand five hundred.

She insisted of course on new furniture and she spent many hours roaming the stores, discussing with the assistants the advantages and disadvantages of that piece and this carpet, and when finally the mortgage was signed and the furnishings duly delivered to the door, she felt that she could not conceivably be any happier. She called the house 'Markova' after the dancer, and they had headed notepaper printed, bearing the address in pale green typeface, 'Markova, Pinewood, Trowbridge Spa, Kent'.

When Ted left at eight in the morning not to return till seven in the evening, she luxuriated for the first time in her life in the sense of being alone. Lying in bed, hearing the latch close, the day seemed to stretch out before her in all its measured, leisured undemanding liberty. In an hour she had done the few household chores, made the bed, vacuum-cleaned and dusted, and for the rest she was left to her own delicious isolation. She could become anyone she wanted to, anyone at all. A mere flick of the gramophone switch and she was dancing *Swan Lake* like Fonteyn, taking curtain call after curtain call for an enraptured audience who showered her with bouquets. She could become Monroe, Marie Antoinette, kept woman, courtesan, princess immured in her solitary tower, prisoner of war, lady of the manor, anyone that her imagination, fed as it was on novellas, movies and romances, could conjure up. On her own with no one to intrude, interrupt, press with the demands of a vulgar world, she made her dreams reality.

In its own perverse way of course the world did intrude, in the shape of postmen, milkmen, neighbours sometimes anxious to pass the time of day in community spirit, to give invitations for tea or morning coffee, and in the evenings of course there were dinners or drinks or parties with Ted's friends. At first she looked forward to them, taking the opportunity to preen herself, to buy a new dress or try a new shade of lipstick or perfume, but in time it began to occur to her, and her fantasy life provided a sharp contrast, that these people were really dull, boring, the conversations were the same, about business, about cars, about the last dance and speculations about the one to come.

She felt at times as if she could scream, shout at them, as if she could shake them into some other kind of life that had more glitter, grace and romance. Even their clothes were drab.

She started making excuses to avoid their company, invented headaches, sudden colds, a migraine that she had read of somewhere that seemed mysterious and aristocratic. So Ted attended gatherings alone, and people, at first solicitous about her, grew apprehensive, suspected that she was being standoffish, and she only the daughter of a bricklayer, and they began to speculate among themselves whether the marriage was cooling. Their sympathies went of course to the husband.

Of this Maureen was ignorant, or if she did suspect she didn't care. She had found a new interest in life. She had taken to travelling up to London once a week to shop, and she looked forward to these excursions with a rare kind of passion. She took the mid-morning train, and alone in the compartment her imagination took off. In the metropolis she wandered down Bond Street and Oxford Street, the grand ballerina incognito. She took tea at Harrods, bought a few purchases and returned on the six o'clock train, compressed with the other commuters. She always set off with the thrilling thought that something exceptional would happen to her, a chance meeting in a train, an acknowledgement in a lift, would transform her life, give it a new and resonant significance.

She thought about having an affair, but there was no one she wanted. The men who had tried to pick her up in London, and there had been several, were cheap, vulgar, importunate. She would not give herself to such as them.

She had in mind someone elegant, cultured, dashing, but the tired faces that assailed her eyes on the train, or that wandered abstractedly and gloomily through the streets, were a far cry from her requirements. They were all so much a part of England, dust and saloon bars, curling railway sandwiches, shiny-seated trousers, shabby paintwork.

Somehow time and disappointment began to erode her dreams. They were still there but relegated to cold storage. She felt listless and morose. A terrible depression settled on her, making her even more lethargic and resentful. She cried for no apparent reason. Simply getting out of bed was a burdensome chore. She kept asking herself again and again, 'What is life for?' And she could think of no answer.

Of course they were more comfortable now. The business was thriving and Ted had achieved his ambition. Hardin's was now a super-scale supermarket, complete with reduced offers, cash registers and the gentle strains of Muzak. They moved to a bigger house on a more exclusive estate with a garage with a folding door that housed last year's model, but still she was daunted by her terrible question.

She thought it was time to have a child and that lifted her, gave her a new focus. She felt it kicking inside her, impetuous to get out. She knitted, bought cots, bought rattles and baubles, designed a nursery in the palest of lavender, read all the books for advice and knowledge. But despite all her preparations, all her precautions, all her ambitions, even all the advancement that medical science has made, the child was stillborn. Something had gone out of her life.

It seemed to her the last final injustice, as though that blind indifferent fate that her reticent father had brooded on so had finally overwhelmed and devoured her. She emerged from the whole harrowing business scarred and defeated.

Ted and his friends rallied round and they took her complicity and exhausted despair as a new turn towards them on her part. She seemed more amiable, more communicative, more friendly. It did not occur to them that these were merely the signals and gestures of one who had given up all hope.

It was a year later that she met David Adler.

Such are the details that I could glean. They suffer of course from compression and from the inadequacies of their writer, but I hope these few words convey some impression at least of that young woman. I can only offer one other insight and this from the pen of Maureen herself. At a later stage I acquired her diary, and perhaps a few random selections might offer a broader perspective. One entry, for example, dates to some three months before she encountered David. It is written in an erratic script in ballpoint pen. The characters shift their direction, sloping now to the left, now to the right. The spelling and punctuation I have retained.

'Got up at nine this morning, all becos of a recorded letter that the postman had for Ted so it didn't seem worth the while to get back, though it was lovely and warm their, Listened to Rdio 1 and they played my favourite …

'Didn't feel like any lunch so I went for a walk round the estate but all the dead leaves depressed me I can't stand Autum it's like a funeral, so I cheered myself up by going to the pictures, the Ritz, saw John and Mary which was lovely with Mia Farow and Dustin Hoffman who reminds me of someone I sat next to at school. He really is fanciable. Wish there was someone like him round here! No such luck … Ted went to one of his functions so I was on my own for a change. Watched tele and had a bath. Paddy came right in the middle. It's two days early I thought I was due the day after tomorrow but I could have made a mistake. Must get some more tampons tomorrow. Brushed hair and bed.'

The second extract was written just the day after she had met David. 'I don't believe it. It's like being in a dream and keep pinching myself to see whether I'll wake up and find that I am. He's gorgeous. Those eyelashes and that voice, and the velvet suit, he's like a dream come true. And when he said he wanted to see me in London I went week at the knees. He couldn't be serious but he left his card and I knew that was his sly way of letting me have his address and he definitely was interested because I could feel that all right – cheaky – but the minute I set eyes on him I new, still it's silly to build hopes up because you can always be let down, but he did say fone and I don't see as how I'd have anything particularly to lose by it, he could always say he was busy or pretend not to be there. Supposing he's got a secretary I'd die if I had to speak to her. It was such a thrill dancing with him. It was completely different from the usual likes round here. To think I've waited all these years. Steady on but still. My stomach's churning just at the thought. Least won't be able to close my eyes all week, because I can't go till Thursday. I feel marvellous. Brushed hair and bed.'

I include the final extract for my own personal reasons of vanity, I suppose. However unpleasant the circumstances were that led to the diary falling into my hands, I have at the same time to look up the entry for the date when she first met me at the penthouse to discover her impression. It is not irrelevant I think. 'Met David's friend George who was really very nice and kept me in fits with his stories about the film world. He's obviously very successful with a lot of money too but I can never understand with people like that with all their advantages how careless they are about certain things in their appearance.

I mean he is quite good looking but it was a bit of a shock when I looked at his hair without him knowing of course, and found it was running alive with dandruff. You'd think someone in his position could use a medicated shampoo.'

Chapter 8

Imagine a cold, clear, November night, the stars like nuggets of quartz. The fields are stiff and phosphorescent with frost. Startled rabbits are sometimes caught in our beam and sometimes startled motorists. I am sitting in the Maserati of David Adler, himself at the wheel. His face, which is barely illuminated by the light from the dashboard, a miraculous spread of spinning dials and quivering needles, is demonic with concentration. The exhaust crackles and coughs through the air.

The road is a winding parallel of asphalt and concrete that we seem to devour. We approach blind corners and then with a sudden touch of brake and a ricochet of gear change, the road adjusts itself and reveals a new direction. I can feel the adhesion of tyre on concrete right through into my seat. Inside, brought to us through the miracle of eight-track stereo cartridges we are enveloped in the rhythms of Creedence Clearwater Revival. From time to time the driver taps out the beat on the steering wheel. Periodically he lights up a cigarette with an electric gadget, housed in the arm rest. He says nothing. There is a fearful determination about him.

We are travelling to Trowbridge Spa. My palms are rivulets of perspiration, clutching my seat, my feet press hard into the floor, my heart trembles every hundred yards.

I am terrified. I glance uneasily at the speedometer and see that on the stretch it registers 105mph. With a sinking desperation I observe ahead the bloodshot rear lights of an articulated lorry droning uphill. In seconds we are behind it, and with merely a blip of a down change, it is a thing of the past, an obstacle overcome. He is humming now to himself.

He had called five days before. 'Maureen would like you to come to a party at her place next Saturday. OK?' I agreed but I had the feeling that *he* wanted me to come and not Maureen. He had no intention of going to a provincial party on his own, I was sure of that, and I was to be there as a protector, or excuse, or some safeguard that could get him out of trouble if he needed it. But I needed no persuasion, for I was already eager for the next instalment of the saga.

The next day after his call the post brought a registered letter containing fifty pounds in ten pound notes. A note said simply, 'Get yourself some clothes and don't nick mine in future.' It was a regular windfall and I certainly had no intention of spending that kind of money on a suit. I found something off the peg in a local shop for fifteen pounds. It was Chinese style and with a shirt that cost fifty bob I showed a profit of just over thirty quid, enough to keep me in comfort along with the supplement of the dole for two months.

Duly, on Saturday at seven-thirty he had called at my flat. The appearance of the car created a stir in the neighbourhood. There could have been no more astonishment as it drew up at the door than if it had been a flying saucer.

The age of affluence had made little impact on Paddington, not I might add through any conservatism or traditionalism on the part of the natives themselves, they would be only too willing to participate, but their employers had other ideas, believing that a sterner puritanism of thrift and hardship was good for the character. Character undoubtedly they have, but not the kind forged in our public schools, more a kind of laissez-faire, a devious independence, light-fingeredness, with a local economy based primarily on the exchange of commodities that have fallen off the backs of lorries. It is safe to assume that as I drew away in the shining gold of the Maserati the neighbours surely concluded that I'd had 'a right tickle'.

As we headed out through south London I had the impression that David was preparing himself for some kind of contest and that the anticipation of it was not entirely unpleasurable. It showed in his face and in his driving which I have tried to describe above, and was finally emphasised when we drove through a tree-lined estate into the gravel drive of a large bungalow. It was something in the way that he slung the car round, braked with a positive finality, and switched off the ignition with a casual flick of the wrist. He leant back in his seat breathing deeply, the adrenalin still pumping from the thrill of the high-speed drive, then after a few seconds, he sucked his lower lip and said, 'OK?' and he was out through the door, slamming it firmly behind him.

There were at least eight other cars in the driveway, and we had to squeeze between them to get to the front porch which was a brick structure encrusted with the dead or dormant branches of a climbing rose. A lantern illuminated the entrance and showed a frosted glass door that was half open. We went in.

My eyes were first accosted by a hallway in which six or seven people had arranged themselves in groups, all with glasses in their hands. Their ages ranged from twenty-five to thirty-five. As we advanced through the door all eyes turned towards us, and those whose position did not favour a view turned to accommodate themselves the better. I had the feeling that we had long been expected and were being given the once-over of assessment, yet no one saw fit to speak to us or even smile. Perhaps it was an uncertainty on their parts, perhaps a communicated nervousness on mine, I do not know, but the whole experience was most embarrassing. I could hear the sounds of an early Beatles LP coming from another room. Having nowhere else to direct my gaze, unless I chose to brazen out the now quite fixed stares, I looked through into what turned out to be the kitchen, harshly lit by a neon strip light and with large black and white tiles on the floor. A table was laden with plates of sausages on sticks, cheeses, salamis, bits of ham, olives, and there were boxes on the floor which contained various bottles of wine and some champagne. One man was leaning against the aluminium sink deep in conversation with another. I wondered if perhaps we had come to the wrong place.

I might have assumed that my uncertainty would not be echoed by my companion, who merely nodded his head and said, 'My name is David Adler. Where's the host please?'

The gathering looked from one to another, hoping in this way to elect a spokesman.

Either a form of lottery worked in some silent way or else a young woman in gold quilted trousers took the responsibility on her shoulders at her own initiative, but at all events she opened her mouth and said 'Oh' and probably, unless I am being over-charitable, would have directed us, had not the host himself, together with his wife, made an appearance from the room where the music was playing. Ted's face beamed with a broad smile of white teeth from ear to ear. He was good-looking I suppose, but I could not help thinking that he reminded me of one of those dummies that are on display in tailor's windows. He had that kind of robot-like posture.

He held out his hand to David. 'I'm glad you got here, old chap. Hope it wasn't too hard to find.'

I was duly introduced, but it was by Maureen that my attention was held. She had that look of sly contentment as she took David's hand. Her cheeks went pink. And as we were ushered into the main room I could not help noticing that she touched his hand and gave it a squeeze.

It was a large grey-carpeted room and the sofa and chairs had been pushed back to the wall to make more space for the guests, who stood in clusters like their colleagues in the hall. Their attention too was firmly upon us, and Ted, only too aware of their interest, played the host like the male lead in a very bad weekly rep.

It was difficult not to notice a large sandstone fireplace that dominated almost the entirety of one wall, its grate occupied by a wrought-iron three-barred fire glowing electrically with red glass coals, and I took up my position there, nowhere else being offered, and waited till Ted placed in my hand a Pimm's No. 1, more packed with fruit and vegetation than I would have thought possible.

I waited, with a certain amount of trepidation I will admit, to be introduced to the assembled throng but in time I realised, much to my relief, that this was not on the agenda, so I busied myself taking in the rest of the room.

It could be described as comfortable, but not I admit entirely to my taste. There was a mahogany bar at the end of the room, well stacked with drink, a marble occasional table, the sofa and two chairs were covered in some sort of furry fabric, and a television whose thirty-inch colour tube must under usual circumstances have vied for attention with the fireplace. That occasion, however, saw it relegated to an inferior position, pushed into a corner, its snout to the wall. What interested me most was an enormous framed photograph of Maureen, a good twenty-four by thirty inches, mounted in gilt, which showed her as the bride of ten years ago. It says a lot I suppose for modern fashions for she looked then, with her hair stiff and permed, her mouth a firm ruby red, much older than the young woman who now talked so animatedly to David in the corner. Ted had left them and was about his task of host, which he did with all the aplomb of an enchanted butler. He joked, he chatted, he poured drink after drink and just at the point when his enthusiasm seemed to wane he bounced back like one of those inflatable toys. In his absence our two lovers moved closer together, and it was not long before she took his hand and led him into a room where I assumed dancing was going on. Indeed, more couples seemed bent on that direction now, for several of them left and made for the sounds of music. All in all perhaps Ted's sterling work was paying dividends and a lot of the earlier chill of the evening was beginning to thaw. I noticed his Pimms No. 1 was making me relax too.

I was not prepared for the young woman who approached me, though I recognised her from her gold quilted trousers as the thwarted leader of the hall, and I was even less prepared for her somewhat rhetorical question which seemed to me to be provocative and over-familiar. She said, 'So you're the writer we've heard so much about.'

I backed a full twelve inches from her. 'Oh have you?'

'Weighing us all up are you? Going to put us in a book?'

She rested her hand on my shoulder, which twitched nervously. 'You can put me in a book any time. I'd like that.' She was obviously drunk, for she slurred her words and giggled. She was not, however, unattractive.

'What's your name?' I asked.

'Vicky,' she said and pouted.

She had large round blue eyes, with a heavy shading of blue on the lids that accentuated the roundness. She was slim with firm little breasts and seemed to wriggle when she talked. Her hair was long and corn-like. As if aware of the assessment I was giving her, she said, 'It's a wig. I'm really brunette, but it's fun to change.'

There was something infuriating about her, so provocative was she and theatrical. She reminded me of something out of a women's magazine, the flirtatious belle of the tennis club.

'I was wondering if it was natural,' I said.

'Oh no I'm dark all over,' and dropped her head to one side and looked at me.

'Well you know what they say,' I said, wondering what it was they did say, but she had lost interest by now, and with a shrug changed her thoughts, like slides in a magic lantern. Whatever passed for ideas in her head turned arbitrarily to the belt that was supporting my trousers. She reached out for it. I noticed she had on a wedding ring.

'I like your belt. It would go well with my trousers. Are you going to let me wear it?'

'Then my trousers would fall down,' I said, patronisingly, as one might to a child.

She giggled, 'I don't mind. Might liven the evening up. Let me have it, please.' She pulled at the belt, then prodded my stomach with her finger. 'They wouldn't fall down. You're too fat.' This seemed to amuse her a lot for she burst into shrieks of laughter and leant against me for support, burying her face in my lapel. When she finally lifted her head I noticed she left patches of make-up behind.

She said, 'I'm surprised to find you alone.'

I caught Ted's eye and he hurried over with a fresh drink. He winked at me rather roguishly, which was unexpected to say the least. Vicky was saying, 'I'd expect someone like you to be with a model. That sort of thing.'

'Then that would be carrying coals to Newcastle,' I said, rather surprised by my own vulgar gallantry.

She smiled. 'Why don't you dance with me then?'

'Why don't I? Why don't you lead the way?'

She took my hand and led me across the room, then pushed through a group of her friends, archly saying, 'Excuse me' and so we came to the 'dance room'.

The most obvious feature here was not the music, which if I remember was Frank Sinatra, or the other couples, but the total darkness the room was plunged in. I could see absolutely nothing and I stumbled around like a man groping for his seat in the cinema. Suddenly I felt an arm and Vicky's voice said, 'Is that you?' and as far as I could tell it was. She put her arms around me and we began to sway to the music. I was reminded of adolescent parties where a room was generally set aside for 'snogging', but that was many years ago and I was surprised to find the comparison apt at a gathering of early middle-aged, or at least adult, married people on a select estate, moreover in Trowbridge Spa, the more so when Vicky began to nestle her head under my chin. There is something unpleasantly disconcerting about being nudged by a mop of artificial hair. I began to wonder whether it might slide off.

In time my eyes adjusted to the darkness and I began to perceive the outlines of other couples, and one dim glance was enough to realise that it was not the dance they were there for. The music provided merely a cover in sound, for as one LP came to an end and before a new one fell in its place, in that brief tuneless interval the whole room seemed to rustle with the noises of sucking lips, murmurs, breathing and the movement of garments, rather like sounds from the undergrowth on a heady summer's night. I confess that I was surprised and shocked in a rather amused way, the more so when I realised that the couple nearest to me was none other than David and Maureen who seemed to have abandoned themselves to each other in an extremely incautious way. I began to fear for their discovery, for Ted was only in the next room, and the provinces being notorious for their gossip I was convinced that at least one evil-minded person would advise him of his wife's misdemeanours. I wondered how I might urge caution upon them without appearing prudish or peremptory. Imagine my surprise then as I stood pondering a strategy in the murk, solicitous only for the well-being of my friends, when Vicky removed her hand from my waist, placed it on my flies and gave my balls a firm and unexpected squeeze. Perhaps a conditioned medical reflex made me cough. She purred like a cat, and as if to extend the metaphor rubbed her face against my chin. There was no doubt in my mind what she was proposing, and any that I might have had was dispelled simply by the tenacious way she held my testicles. It was as if she was weighing them, assessing them, cupped in the palm of her hand, like a judge at a prize show. It seemed churlish not to draw her closer to me and find her all too accommodating mouth in the dark, which I did, mainly to find a breathing, or as it turned out non-breathing, space, to consider the full implications of her gesture. She was after all a married woman and her husband was presumably in the vicinity. On the other hand, like our neighbours, she seemed in no way deterred. On the contrary, the way she ran her wet little tongue along the inside of my lip and pressed her prominent pelvic bone into my penis, which Lazarus-like was raising himself from the dead, made me think that she was desirous of me to fuck her then and there. I was not quite sure of local etiquette, but it seemed well within the bounds of possibility. I could at least signal my intention, so placing a hand between her quilted thighs I began to massage somewhere in the region of her clitoris, which aroused in her even more forceful passions. She bit the lobe of my ear really quite hard, then whispered into it in an explosive rush, 'Not now. Later.'

What she had in mind I was not quite sure, but in her estimation at least something had been settled, for she removed her arms from me and made for the door, and other couples in the room also began to break up, either on signal or out of a kind of intuition. I wondered if my experience in that room had been replicated several times over.

In the drawing room I lost her. She skipped across the grey carpet and went up to a man sporting a bandanna and Mexican-style moustache. She kissed him affectionately on the cheek and they began conversing. I formed the impression that this Zapata of the provinces was none other than her husband. They had a familiar manner with each other.

Ruminating somewhat over the extraordinary, for me that is, events of the evening, I decided to take my distended penis to the lavatory, if only to relieve it of some pressure of accumulated alcohol. I steered my way into the hallway where I found a likely door and pushed it open. My action seemed to cause a great deal of disquiet to a gaunt young man of twenty-five who had propped himself against the frame of the open front door and was vomiting epically onto the outside porch. He was obviously a person of some resource and thoughtfulness for, drunk though he was and in considerable distress, he had the presence of mind to wave at me and shake his head, saying, 'That's the sauna. The bog's through there.'

Having delivered me this advice, he threw forward his head and retched out a flow of vinous spew. I nodded my thanks and found the appropriate door.

Examining my blood-flecked eyes in the tinted bathroom mirror, I went over certain details of the gathering in my mind. They were mostly in their thirties and all without exception married. They had all brought their spouses, yet they all necked with impunity with other people in a darkened room, making extremely erotic suggestions. It followed that either they were all blind drunk, which was not the case apart from the unfortunate in the hall, or they were all blind, which statistically was improbable, or, and this seemed the most likely, they were all colluding with each other's promiscuity. I had not experienced this cultural phenomenon before, though I had heard of it through the agencies of our more salacious newspapers, and I came to the conclusion that such was I witnessing.

My return to the drawing room confirmed my diagnosis, for the entire assembly were gathered there. Ted, in his role of host and master of ceremonies, was moving from man to man and taking from each a car key which he deposited in a tin box, on which had been scrawled in biro the words 'Swop box'. The company were all extremely jovial and there was a good deal of laughter and many suggestive remarks were made. Once the keys had been duly collected, the box was placed in the centre of the room. It was now the ladies' turn. Each selected a key from the box at random, though I suspect certain arrangements had been made by some pairs in advance. When all the keys had been thus redistributed, the owner of each was found and, thus newly paired, the couples would drive off to the lady's home where they would spend the night together. It was now midnight. There were various laughing protests, jovial complaints, a raucous comment or two, but on the whole the operation was conducted with maximum efficiency and speed, and it was obvious to this observer that it ran smoothly from constant repetition. They gathered their coats and with gay promises to see each other on the morrow they wished each other good night.

Vicky did come up to me, and I don't think I flatter myself when I say that her face showed signs of disappointment. She said sadly, 'Next time bring your own car,' and was gone.

I reflected glumly that in these modern times even for sex you need a driving licence. I suddenly found myself alone with just the ashtrays and the glasses and the debris. Outside, their cars roared away, the sound of one facetious horn challenging the night. I wondered how David had reacted to the evening and what he was doing now, but since there was no sign of him or Ted, I assumed they were about their business. I took off my jacket and my shoes and, there being nothing else for me to do, stretched out on the sofa and fell asleep, too tired and drunk and bemused to think any more.

Chapter 9

I awoke with a dry throat, dull eyes and cramp in my left arm – Aurora, the dawn. A few blinking seconds confirmed my location and the reality of the events of the night before. I was sweaty from the storage heaters that had flushed out their cheap-tariff heat in the early hours of the morning. I sat up on the sofa and wriggled my stockinged toes and would have buried my head in my hands had not my attention been diverted by the sound of a car drawing up, followed by the bang of a door. I pulled aside a curtain and observed Ted, whistling quietly to himself, crunching his way, unshaven from a night of alternative passion, up the drive of the house that he had slaved and paid for. Behind him a weak early November sun gave a misty sheen to the damp lawns, and the shrubbery, planted with such military precision, glistened with the traceries of dewy cobwebs. A bird warbled in some distant tree.

He came cautiously into the room to confirm my presence, waking or sleeping, and finding me struggling into my jacket, still in my socks (what absurd guilts I feel in other people's houses), he smiled in his roguish way and enquired, 'Did you sleep all right?'

I assured him I had and forced my right foot into a resisting shoe. Under his arm he was carrying the newspapers that he had picked up at the door, and these he placed on the marble table, before beginning to pick up ashtrays which he piled methodically one on top of the other. I rushed to his assistance.

'It's all right,' he said with that reassuring tone of the tradesman. 'I don't like to see the place looking like a pigsty.' I had a suspicion that he had placed me in the role of pig.

'How about some breakfast?' The way he raised his eyebrows suggested something discreet, confidential almost. I nodded my acceptance. 'I'll rustle something up in the kitchen. You read the papers. There's no sense disturbing Maureen and co. just yet,' he added with a wink and disappeared, balancing the ashtrays like a juggler.

He amazed me. What was it with this polite and ever smiling caricature, who bustled around like a ship's steward, albeit first-class deck, while his wife lay in the arms of her lover in an adjacent room? How was it with all of them at that party?

Had a whole cultural revolution somehow passed me by, or was this some new expression of social malaise, an emptiness, a boredom? Was it some grotesque aping of what was thought to be trendy in the swinging city? Or was it some genuine sophistication, some imaginative attempt to come to terms with the problems of staleness and the wanings of sexual desire in marriage? But if so, it was all so formalised and passionless. And what price did he pay for those smiles? How could those brown bright eyes not hint at any disturbance? Where was his anger placed, where did it hide? Was he beyond jealousy? Was he beyond feelings? How could he now be frying eggs and bacon, percolating coffee, for their aroma was now sensual in my nostrils, popping bread into an electric toaster which popped back at him brown and warm, humming contentedly to himself? How could he leave his bed to the lusts of a rival for a whole night? And furthermore how could he arrive the next morning with a shirt as impeccably white as when he had first put it on?

I confess that I could find no satisfactory explanations. The newspapers that he had left me gave evidence of a dull, conservative, even reactionary mind, but there was nothing surprising in that. Most men in his position and occupation are like that, reflecting merely their own commercial interests. They are the kind, I will admit, that normally I avoid like the plague. We have very little in common other than mutual suspicion and hostility. But Ted had revealed a side to his nature that I could not but be astonished by.

While preparing breakfast he had managed to shave and it was a smooth and lotioned face that popped round the door and announced that breakfast was ready in the kitchen, if I didn't mind. He was wearing a blue-striped, butcher's-style apron, over freshly changed wheat-coloured trousers and check shirt.

The conversation at table was predictable enough, and I won't bore you with a verbatim account of it, for it offers no new insights into his character. He asked questions about my work, seemed interested and convinced by my lies (I was beginning to find my act wearisome, but it now seemed that I was saddled with it); he wanted to know where I lived and remarked that there were a lot of 'sambos' in Paddington, said what a good place Trowbridge Spa was and what a good crowd his friends were. I add only in his favour that he was an excellent cook of bacon and eggs.

He was expanding on the theory that strikes and high wages were bringing the economy of the country to its knees when the door opened and Maureen came in. She was wearing a long nylon dressing gown and her hair was uncombed. Her face was puffy and I had the feeling that she had spent most of the night in tears and without sleep. I guessed that she was alone, and a glance through the window confirmed this, for David's car was not there. She went to the table and poured herself a cup of coffee.

Ted assessed the situation immediately. His cheery 'Morning, love' was a good-natured formality, but he had the presence of mind to realise that his wife wanted to be left alone. He pushed back his chair and announced, 'I think I'll play a few holes of golf to clear the head. I'll be back for lunch.' Then he left the room and some seconds later I caught a glimpse of him, his clubs on his shoulder, walking to the car. One turn of the ignition key and the Rover took him off.

She sat at the table, a tall bedraggled unhappy thing, staring vacantly into her cup as if it might deliver up oracular advice with its vapours. I felt uneasy in this situation and wondered in what way I could console her or relieve some of her obvious anxiety and distress. I thought perhaps that if I asked her what had happened she might feel confident enough to talk, but before I could speak she pre-empted me with a long sigh and said, shaking her head, 'It was a terrible mistake.'

I fumbled in my pocket for a packet of cigarettes and offered her one, which she took and placed in her mouth. She then seemed to forget about it and it stayed there for some minutes while slowly she rubbed her forehead, lost in some new depression.

'Do you want to talk about it?' I finally suggested.

She appeared to make some conscious effort to draw herself together, for she lit the cigarette and said, 'I think I've ruined everything.'

'Was he angry?' I offered a question in the way that a rescuer might point out ledges on a cliff face to a trapped climber, hoping she would reach for them one by one.

'Yes,' she replied.

'What with?'

'Oh, the whole party. All that awful crowd. They do all that swapping business every week. I never have anything to do with it. It seems childish to me.' With the light behind her and her dark hair ruffled she looked no more than a gawky child.

'I only asked him here, so I could see him.' The injustice of it seemed to affect her the more, and her lower lip quivered as though she might burst into tears. 'I didn't mean anything by it. I was just pleased to see him.' And this time she broke completely. Her head dropped into her hands and her shoulders shook with sobbing. It was obvious that she was incapable of giving a coherent account of the night, though I had formed certain obvious conclusions myself. I got up from my chair and went round to her to try and comfort her. I put my arms lightly on her shoulders to reassure her, and she turned suddenly, desperately, to me, her arms clasped around my waist and her face buried in my stomach. She sobbed like that for a while and I could feel her tears and her face warm and wet through my shirt. I stroked her hair.

In time she rubbed her cheeks across my belly as if to dry her eyes, and then she looked up at me, a picture of such tragic misery, the tears still welling onto her inflamed lids. She said, 'Please tell him I'm sorry.' And then desperately again like a grieving child, 'Make it all right with him will you, please?' The last was a heart-rending plea.

But the outburst must have given a certain necessary therapy, for she got up from the table and over to the sink, where she pulled off a strip of kitchen tissue from a large roll and blew her nose hard into it.

I doubted if my continued presence there would have helped her in any way. I got the impression that she would prefer me gone, if only so that I might get about my task the more quickly, so I muttered words to the effect that I would do my best for her and suggested that I ought to be going. She said, 'But how will you get back?' and I assured her that there were ways.

'Well, let me look up the train times,' she said, but I declined her offer and left her with the last reassurance that I would do my best.

Outside it was deceptively cold. The sun had been falsely assessed from the inside warmth of central heating, and without an overcoat I shivered. I walked briskly down the avenue and as luck would have it got on a convenient bus that took me to the centre of the town. I was torn by an enchanted curiosity to explore the streets of my childhood, to see again the house that I had spent many happy years in. In fact the bus dropped me close by the very street and I had to walk down it, but apart from an impression that it was much shorter (how deceptive distances are to the eye of a child!) I took in really very little. My thoughts were too overcast by the memory of that unhappy girl who coloured and dominated all my impressions. I strolled casually by the house, feeling only how much older I was and in reality how far removed from it. Hunching my shoulders against the wind, and regretting that my Mao jacket had no collar, I took the first Green Line bus back to London.

It took me several days to contact David and when I did I pressed upon him how anxious she was and how eager to make amends. After some discussion he agreed to contact her and this he did. I felt glad that in some small way I had been able to do something to give her peace of mind.

His account of the evening was of course much fuller than hers, and he told it not without a sense of outrage and irritation and, to my surprise, disapproval. He had in fact been shocked and disgusted by it and blamed her quite heartlessly. And even though I hastened to assure him of the contrary, I doubt whether he was really convinced, and I don't think that their affair ever really recovered from it.

It seems that he found the party enjoyable enough, even though from a position of a metropolitan superiority and irony. He was curious about the other guests and assessed them in the sharp and instant way that had made him such a success at his own money-making racket, but they in no way impinged upon his genuine pleasure in seeing Maureen. If anything, it added a new spice that all eyes were upon him. He treated the necking sessions with an appropriate irony and had joked quietly with her in the dark about it all.

It was only when the matter of the car keys was introduced that he began to feel uneasy, and as the ritual played itself out before his eyes he got angrier and angrier. My attention was fixed too much on the formalities of the game and did not notice that he had left the room before the proceedings arrived at their prurient conclusions. Maureen herself had not noticed his departure and it was only when she tried to retrieve his key that she discovered he had gone. She set out immediately after him. To the assembled group, and I suspect I may have been guilty of this too, it was seen only as evidence of a passionate impetuosity on both their parts.

She found him, white with rage, alone in the bedroom. He turned on her immediately and cruelly. He accused her of trying to make a fool of him 'in front of these hicks. Who do you think I am? Some small-time, saloon bar womaniser? Does it look as though it's my scene? When I want a gang-bang with a bunch of semi-retarded petit bourgeois shopkeepers, I'll say so. Don't you ever try and force me into a situation like that again. You stick to the provinces, baby. You get fucked every Saturday night by the old man's best friend and giggle about it next day at the golf club. But don't you try and involve me in it.'

She stood there dumbly, hanging her head, not daring to look into his face, whose very coldness and venom seem to wither her insides. She was absolutely overwhelmed by the brute force of his invective and totally unprepared for it. She had never seen him like this before, she had never before met anyone like this, who hurled abusive accusations at her, the very eloquence of which made even a reply impossible. She was terrified and ashamed and humiliated and what was more she could say nothing. Her brain was like a wordless desert, not one phrase or explanation in sight. Her tongue was locked in her throat, and her own silence, and now his threatening waiting silence, paralysed her all the more. He heard her stomach gurgle like a distant tank.

At length he said, 'Don't you think you owe me some sort of explanation?'

But there was nothing she could say, except that she was sorry, that she loved him, had been so happy with him all evening, that the rest of that dreadful crowd had for her been merely dim shapes in the background that his very presence had blotted out, that she wanted him to take her to bed, to make love to her as though nothing had happened. Yet she couldn't even raise her head to look at him, much less speak.

Suddenly he grew impatient. The whole affair seemed in any case so idiotic. It was impossible to know what he had ever seen in her, this stupid, ignorant girl who stood in front of him more like a guilty adolescent than a grown woman. It had just been an aberration on his part, a whim, a fantasy. The living reality in front of him dispelled all illusions. He just had to get out. He muttered, 'What the fuck am I doing here anyway?' and walked out of the room.

She felt too numb even to follow him. She heard merely the door slam and then his car start, and then an angry sound as the tyres ground into the gravel. She threw herself onto the bed and sobbed.

He drove to London and spent the night with an old girl friend who seemed glad and surprised to see him. In his mind the whole thing seemed settled and finished.

It is difficult to know whether my intervention changed his mind or whether in the few days' absence from her he had begun to miss her of his own accord. If the former, I was glad to have served as a transmission mechanism for their reconciliation. Undoubtedly a lot of his anger and outrage was the outcome of wounded vanity and a sense of his own self-importance. An element of paranoia was also present but he reacted so vehemently, I think, out of a certain jealousy and this was some measure of the depth of his feelings for her or, if not her, then what she represented to him in his mind. It would not be the first time that a man was angry and disappointed when his dream object exhibited some behaviour or trait outside the rosy confines that fantasy imposes. It is a permanent hazard for the idealist.

But they continued their association every Thursday, and to all intents and purposes it seemed the same. Maureen was obviously thankful for this and anxious to wipe out her former mistake. She never invited him home again. And David found he had little time to brood, for his attention now turned to business matters which kept him more than occupied.

The initial research into the Spa project was now complete and David met the town planners for approval of his scheme.

He proposed a whole new shopping complex of covered arcades, and an auditorium-cum-theatre. Above the theatre would rise, a full twenty-two storeys in height, an office block of reinforced concrete and glass, the size and scope of which the town had never seen. He promised, as a gesture to the arts and to augment the cultural activity of the town, to donate the theatre free of charge to the civic authorities, thus repaying in some small way, he said with a modest smile, the debt he owed to his home town.

The committee discussed his proposals and were not unimpressed. His designs seemed very much in harmony with their own architectural and commercial aspirations for the town, and confirmed that private enterprise still had a role to play in the future of town planning. It had the added advantage of enabling them to concentrate their attention and resources, without an increase in rates – a point not without relevance in an election year – on the Spa ring road scheme, a visionary and futuristic concept that would nestle the town in the spanning arms of a thriving, circular, five-lane highway. These twin proposals could only bring prosperity and contentment to all, it was felt.

There was some disagreement over the matter of the theatre, for some held that this catered for a minority taste and was therefore perhaps an unnecessary extravagance, though a generous one on the part of its donor. These objections were brushed aside, however, when it was explained that the auditorium could be readily adapted to meet the requirements of dances and conferences which could only bring fresh commercial interest to the town. The vote confirmed a unanimous agreement and the committee assured David that he could rely on their fullest co-operation. They wished him every success in his venture, and readily granted planning permission.

It must have been while these heady discussions were taking place that I received a letter from Maureen. It read:

Dear George. Just a line to let you know how much I appreciate all you did and said and I am happy to say that everything between me and David is now just fine. And like it was before. I really am grateful for what you did and like you to know that if there's anything I can do for you just let me know. I would be only too pleased. Vicky keeps asking after you. You made a big hit there. If you'd like me to say something you only have to ask, though perhaps she's not your type and you probably think it's a cheek on my part even suggesting it, but I didn't see there was any harm in letting you know.

Anyway, I won't ramble on because I'm sure you must be busy. So I'll close for now, with a thank you for all you've done.

Maureen.

Chapter 10

He wanted me to come to Ireland for Christmas. I was to fly over with Maureen to Cork Airport and he would meet us there. Ted was to be away the four days of the festive season on a golfing holiday-cum-tournament. He must have known by now of her affair with David, for she was not particularly discreet and he must have recognised at that unfortunate party and its aftermath that there was more to their relationship than a Saturday swap. At that stage I could only guess at his reasons, but it seemed that there was more than an element of complicity on his part, as to spend four days on windy greens and iron-hard fairways is well beyond the limits of sporting enthusiasm.

There was some discussion as to whether I should bring a girl and for a while I was somewhat uneasy that the bold Vicky would be suggested as a likely candidate, but fortunately for me family ties exert a stronger pull than promiscuity at that season of the year, and she was to spend it with her husband and two children round the tree with yule log blazing. I explained that I did not feel in particular need of female companionship and the discussion was finally dropped. To me it was something of a relief to get out of London at this time, especially since David was footing the entire bill, air tickets and all. Christmas is always a moment of anxiety for me as the only alternative to my barren and cold room, where there is always the possibility of starvation since the local cafe closes its steamed-up and welcoming doors, is to share the festivities somewhat glumly with my ageing parents, who still sport crackers and paper hats at dinner before settling down to the marathon task of twenty-two hours' TV viewing without respite, save for the occasional meagre offer of port or sherry or tea.

So I set off to Cromwell Road to catch the Heathrow bus in unusually high spirits, rather like a prisoner on temporary release from Wormwood Scrubs. The weather was not too bad and I had avoided the flu. The traffic in the streets had a purposeful air, rather than the irritable lethargy of mere commuting. The terminal was jam-packed with eager faces. all were in their new going away clothes, trolleys piled high with luggage and brightly wrapped presents. BEA, Air France and Alitalia announced the departure of their flights in the icy way that tannoys have. And there was I in it all with my battered little suitcase with its worn strap and a crisp new ticket in my pocket. Jingle bells already!

It seemed somehow very appropriate that she should be standing by the large glittering Christmas tree in the departure lounge, in black leather boots and bright red coat and hat ... She smiled and waved her hand as soon as she saw me. There was something really marvellously warm and open about her, and I felt glad that I was travelling with her. Just spontaneously I put my arms round her and kissed her lightly on the cheek, and she giggled and said, 'Fresh' and kissed me back.

On the bus we said very little to each other, just an occasional remark from her about something she'd seen from the window. I asked if she had been to Ireland before and we discovered that for both of us it was the first time. But the silence between us was not the kind that isolated us from each other, rather it was an expression of a shared excitement, a rather childlike sense of adventure. It was obvious that she was eager to be with David again and the way she peered out of the window in the bus and later in the plane showed a kind of impatience that registered passing fields and clouds and sea merely as landmarks in her progress to him. Once strapped into my safety belt, however, my silence sprang from another source. Quite simply, I am terrified of flying. My ears strain for every change and nuance of engine noise, convinced that each is the signal that announces our lurching, sickening, uncontrollable spiral down into the icy sea, or else is the last mechanical hint before the apocalyptic explosion that hurls our dismembered bodies to all four corners of the horizon. Our Christmas special flight had more than its fair share of nuns who knitted their rosaries at every bump and judder of turbulence, demonstrating a profound lack of faith either in our soft-tongued and over-patronising Captain O'Keep or in the Almighty himself, I was not sure which. For a moment I did imagine with a morbid kind of pleasure the magical spectacle of these black-cowled women blasted suddenly heavenwards like buckshot from a gun, but it was a fleeting diversion and a sudden dip in flight returned me to my palpitating and sweaty senses. There is something unnatural and hazardous in being suspended some twenty thousand feet above the ground.

He was waiting all smiles at the airport. His few days in the country had added a colour to his cheeks. He was dressed in a white Aran sweater, wellington boots, a navy blue donkey jacket and to my astonishment a navy blue sailing cap. I began to believe that a fishing trawler would be waiting for us in the car park rather than the black mini with its darkened glass windows. Maureen threw her arms round his neck with a little skip, and he grinned at me rather sheepishly and prodded me on the shoulder and said in the manner of a tour courier, 'Welcome to Ireland.'

Outside the airport building, I peered up anxiously into the sky in part to give a vote of thanks for my safety, but mainly to confirm whether mist and torrential rain were imminent, for that was the kind of weather I had been led to expect of this country. To my surprise and relief, the clouds were white, buffeted boisterously, it's true, by a gusty wind, but shifting across the bluest of skies presided over by a confident sun. It was 24 December after all and the weather seemed to me a good omen for the next four days.

We got into the car, Maureen in the front, me wrestling with my constricted legs in the miniature back, and in that way we set off for his away-from-it-all home.

It involved a drive of over sixty miles and an extremely pleasant journey it turned out to be. He was in very high spirits, talkative, joking and laughing and in front of me they seemed very close as she leaned towards him, and he, from time to time, stroked her knee and thigh. He obviously enjoyed showing us the country, as if he felt very close to it, something that was very privately his and he was eager to demonstrate his feelings and make us share in them. He pointed out rivers, ruined towers, small villages, but all the time he kept promising, 'This is nothing. Wait till we really get to West Cork' and Maureen was a perfect foil for his enthusiasm, for she pointed and gasped and said 'Look at that' and 'Isn't it lovely' and turned round to me for confirmation, 'Don't you think?'

We were climbing a hill which curved away at the top to the right. To its left was a lay-by and he swung the car into it unexpectedly and stopped. He pointed with his arm and said, 'Look at that.'

Something in his tone could not but make one feel that the view he indicated was something that he personally in some Godlike way had had a hand in creating, but perhaps this is merely churlish on my part, for what lay before us in all its green, dipping and rocky surface was a most magnificent landscape. The earth fell down a gentle slope into the arms of the Atlantic, which was flinging itself at the rocks on the coastline in explosions of bright, white spray. The eye took in the great sweeping undulations of a coast that curled its way in volcanic coves and bays to the furthermost horizon. And the sea itself was broken by myriad islands, some small, barren and rocky, that gulls and cormorants wheeled and dived over, others green and gorsey where cows chewed and farm houses were scattered. And the colours were so amazing, so rich and varied, from the brilliant turquoise of the sea itself to the dissolving purple haze of heather, bracken like rust, slate-blacks and blues of rock face, the soft grey green of lichen and the bright emerald of moss. We all stood silent and breathless, leaning against the well of the lay-by, the wind drawing our clothes around us, and when finally by walking back to the car he gave the signal that the experience was finished, he looked at both Maureen and me with an expression that was both contented and cocky as if to say, 'What did I tell you?'

We drove off, Maureen and I still mesmerised by the view, turning our heads until the veering of the road hid it from our sight. But freshened by the extravagant beauty and the assault of the wind, I felt the car was warmer and more protective and that all three of us were very close.

He slotted a cassette into the player and suddenly the car echoed with the sound of the choir of King's College Chapel singing the Christmas carol service. It was undoubtedly a coup on his part, timed to perfection. The clear soprano voices of the boys not only blended with the scenery, the movement of the car, the glint of sunshine on the windows, but added a whole new magical dimension. It released in me a whole flood of nostalgia, for however hardened an atheist I am, the singing of carols reduces me to a sentimental pulp. And in the car I don't think I was alone in the feeling, for Maureen, quietly and uncertainly at first, began singing in a rather thin breathy contralto, and then David joined her, and soon all three of us were singing at the tops of our voices not altogether tunefully 'Hark the herald angels sing', while the sea endlessly buffeted the passing coast.

And in this way we arrived at the house.

It was situated spectacularly by the sea, overlooking a blue natural harbour, that lay beneath a tall craggy face of cliff. To the west was a point beyond which the Atlantic was swollen with angry flecked breakers, but to the east all was a tranquil blue shifted only by the tides, on which rocked and bobbed gulls and puffins and birds whose names I do not know. Occasionally the whiskered ball-shaped face of a seal would rise enquiringly to the surface. Just beneath the cliff on the far shore was a small jetty where local fishing boats moored, and by the jetty, landlocked, the local bar and all-provision store.

The gardens were sculptured – perhaps the best word I can find – descending in rocky and grassy terraces down to a small cove where his three boats were moored, tugging at their orange lengths of rope and matching buoys. The launch was painted black and turquoise and stood in bright contrast to the ultramarine of a dinghy and the purple of a skiff. The water lapping round them acted as a natural setting to their moving coloured forms. Nor was it simply an accident of nature. The arrangement of shape and colour was deliberately chosen, the inspired work of an architect friend. All was a contrived harmony and I felt personally ill at ease in it, for while admiring it I felt that by merely standing there I was spoiling the composition which had no need of the human form, much less the unaesthetic bundle that I comprised. By the boats was the boat house, a long low black building, that was allotted to me for the duration, but lest I give the impression that some cold barren garage had been given me, there being no room at the inn of the house, let me hasten to add that its interior was spectacular in both design and comfort. All was stripped wood and fur rugs, and sofas and paintings and multicoloured walls. The wash of water caressed the ears.

But the boat house was a mere bagatelle compared with the main structure that stood a little higher up in a garden of rocks and fuchsia and soft lawns and wild heather. Maureen ran from room to room like an excited child, her breath literally taken away.

It is difficult to give a real impression of its interior, and an inventory would bore you, but it was like I suppose walking through the pages of a certain kind of fashion magazine. It was obviously the work of an interior designer, colourful, clever, contrived, using different textures and surfaces and shapes and levels, but its designer obviously understood the psychology of his employer well, for though it showed nothing really of the personal taste of David, it nevertheless embodied the essence of what he would like to be. It's a somewhat sophistical distinction but a true one nevertheless. There was just the right hint of Hollywood, of vulgarity, of ambition and aspiration. And it was obvious that David himself recognised these hints for he fitted into this interior with all the strutting pleasure of a leading actor surveying his set for the first time. He felt it and he saw that it was good.

But for all this, it was a cheerful atmosphere, comfortable, a turf fire blazed brightly in the stone hearth, wafting its own peaty incense into the room. From the kitchen came the smell of beef that an Irish housekeeper was preparing. David poured us drinks. Maureen said, 'Can I see upstairs?'

He led the way like a guide, up a wide cedar staircase into the bedroom. It was here I think that the designer had gone too far, that his discretion had given way and he had slipped over into too heavy an irony. For the room was like a tent, striped fabric hanging down from the crossbar, as it were, of the room, draping down the walls to the floor. A large picture window looked over the wilder aspects of the ocean and by it was a neat mahogany and brass desk with a huge shiny leather chair. Apart from a cradled globe of the world, the only other piece of furniture was a vast high bed, so high that it had to be mounted from a stepping block.

There was a certain military feel to the room (Napoleon on campaign) but this might merely be the prejudiced impression of one whose taste is of a more modest order. Certainly my reservations were not shared by Maureen, who gave a delighted gasp and flung herself onto the bed at which I left the room discreetly, allowing them to renew each other's acquaintance.

Over lunch we drank a good deal of wine and ate beef and jacket potatoes. The conversation varied and was mainly the work of David, who told stories of how he had bought the house, how he had fallen in love with the place, what the local inhabitants were like, details that would be of marginal interest to relate in full. Suffice it to say that he talked with a kind of self-mockery, with an element of playing down his enthusiasms, that gave to his delivery a sharp ironic edge. And my role in this? Reserved in a way, cautious, not always declaring myself. Part of this might be explained by the real disparity of interests between us, which to meet head on would merely result in unprofitable conflict, but mainly I held myself back because to be with David was to accept the domination of his personality. He could not really conduct intercourse in any other way. Tell him a story and his eyes begin to wander, his attention drift, his foot begins to tap. He is compelled to initiate, to conduct, to control. When he listens it is solely for his benefit, to extract what he needs and use it to his advantage at a later stage. He conducts his business in this manner, with the confidence and primarily contempt of the autocrat.

114

For relaxation and amusement he is at heart a performer, a man who needs an audience to measure himself by. Some basic lack of aggressiveness made me capitulate to these demands. And if you ask me why I don't find him entirely intolerable, overbearing and arrogant, I can only say that he's genuinely interesting and amusing and entertaining ... And furthermore when he's at his most domineering he's also at his weakest.

And Maureen, what of her? Sitting at table, a dark blackberry line of wine on her lower lip, holding her knife and fork in the most ludicrously 'refined' fashion, launching her implements dart-like into the bloody red beef, her little finger cocked, how did she transcend her uncertain social pretensions so that she was not merely a figure of fun? How was it that in spite of all this one warmed to her? What was her quality, for quality she had, and why could he become so inflamed and impatient with desire for her, as he did towards the end of lunch with such sudden and compelling urgency? I began to wonder how much art and calculation were concealed in her very simplicity. It was hard to tell and I watched her as closely as I could. Or was it just the force of his own inner fantasy life that needed merely a catalyst to be released, however arbitrary and unknowing that catalyst was. At all events he made it clear that he had pressing engagements with her, and with the most peremptory of farewells, he took her hand and led her upstairs.

There being no further business at hand for me, I walked

outside into the garden and from there followed the line of the bay. The air was fresh and began to clear my wine-fuddled brain. I scrambled over rocks and peered into the clear water of pools where seaweed swayed like the vegetation of a prehistoric age, crabs scuttled and tiny fish like glass splinters cavorted in sudden flashing movements. I sat on the end of a small promontory and watched the gulls bicker like fishwives over a bundle of floating refuse.

What was it with those two? Perhaps I do her an injustice to say that her motives seemed clearer to me. That she should be drawn to him is not difficult to appreciate, given the conditions of her life, her own thwarted if immature dreams which were released in the dashing charisma of David. But for him, young, good-looking, successful and voracious enough to take by the scruff of the neck anything that took his fancy, why her? He could have, has had and probably still has, any number of stunningly attractive women, but that is not really the question or the problem. That he should choose a Maureen is comprehensible along certain fantasy lines, which I have tried to suggest at an earlier point of this account. The problem was not that he saw her, but that he continued to see her, and with such eagerness. It is true that their encounters were brief and well regulated so as to minimise the deadly threat of boredom that afflicts so many relationships of this kind. On the surface at least there was little that could be detected that could bring them together, for they seemed to have so little in common. He had a sharp, critical and exploitative intelligence, whereas she grasped only dimly at concepts and seemed motivated by the most naive of hopes and trusts.

Obviously a deep mutual sexual attraction was at the centre of their relationship and it is difficult to speculate on the components that go into its make-up, for it is so entwined and underlaid with the elements of fantasy that are established at such an early stage of our development. However firm or rounded the arse, curvacious the breasts, capacious the orifice, it is not simply these physical attributes that sustain desire. They merely provide the objective outlines that fantasy breathes form and substance and life into. And fantasy is what one must plumb when trying to express an opinion. I offer inconclusive speculations merely, but I wondered whether it was not that helplessness in her that excited him, that ready vulnerability.

And it is true to say that Maureen so often saw herself in the role of victim, and yet, parodoxically, like all victims she had displayed in her life a ruthlessness and heartlessness in pursuit of her own aims. Witness her poor father and the cruelly cuckolded Ted.

But victims in this world are not hard to find and this offers no real explanation of why he selected her. Suggest also that he had a yearning for what he might have been, or that beneath the exterior of the powerful man of capital there lurked a lonely misfit who found in her arms a lost identity, then you have possibly a not inaccurate formula but no more.

We must leave a certain area of mystery, or call it if you will a lack of information on the part of this author, but all in all we must say that if they could give each other the lineaments of gratified desire, then who am I to enquire? What worried me was how long it would last and what terrible price would be paid for the breakup, for I was sure that their affair was only the outburst of a moment, and had no perspective on the future.

The sun had retired with an uncharacteristic modesty. There were no fireworks, shimmerings, volcanic streakings. It was merely there one minute and had gone. I stumbled my way through the dusk and up to the house, where I found Maureen lying on a sofa and David at table. There was silence between them, and the look in his face that suggested impatience, as though he had been waiting for me to return for some time. Before him was a scrabble board, its pieces laid out in preparation. I had barely passed through the door and into the room when he said with an emphasis that excluded all real choice, 'Do you want to play?'

Chapter 11

The birthday of Our Lord came dull and damp. An all-shrouding mist hung over the waters and reduced visibility to little more than ten yards. From the boat house where I had spent a not over-restful night, the house was invisible. I pulled on a thick sweater that I found in a drawer and drifted through the mist, looking and feeling like Hamlet's father's ghost.

There was no one about and I assumed that the lovers were still abed. The fire that burnt reassuringly in the hearth was the early work of the housekeeper, who had since left for Mass. I headed for the kitchen and boiled an undemanding little brown egg.

The remainder of the morning I spent pleasurably, alone in a book by the said fire and it was not really until noon that I heard sound of movement from above and Maureen descended the stairs in nylon and made for the kitchen. Passing me she smiled and said, 'Merry Christmas,' and went on, 'Talk about lazy, he's still half asleep and wants a cup of tea.' She floated away on her long supple legs.

Tea drunk, and followed by baths, it was not until nearly two p.m. that the couple finally descended with solicitous enquiries of my welfare. Their mood seemed jovial, and after David had established his dominance and ownership of the room by piling high the fire with peat, he went over to the radiogram and began to play a collection of seventy-eights of Danny Kaye. He has a pleasant voice and the tunes define for me and David likewise a period, and it was not long before we were discussing over enormous whiskies memories of the fifties, reminiscences that seemed to have no interest for Maureen, who read a magazine and intervened once only with a meaningful complaint that 'It's a pity there is no tree.'

At three-thirty the housekeeper reappeared and by four we were eating turkey and pudding and were drunk as lords.

David when drunk becomes increasingly sardonic. A physical change seems to take place in him for his face seems to inflate like a bladder and his eyes narrow with hostility and aggression. His voice too gets loud. The characteristic that he has when 'normal' of domination extends into manipulation and he takes an obvious pleasure in belittling those around him. The change in him is usually sudden, as it was on this occasion, and the period of good-natured boyishness, when he jokes and giggles and makes positive physical contact with you, slapping, knee patting, vanishes with one strange extra mouthful that sends him over the top.

He announced suddenly by slapping on the table, 'It's time for me to play Santa Claus.'

'Presents, you mean?' said Maureen, her eyes bright in anticipation.

'Presents is exactly what I mean,' he said, and levering himself heavily out of his chair he directed himself to a chest of drawers, opened a cupboard and pulled out three brown wrapped parcels. Maureen looked across at him excitedly and nibbled at her thumbnail.

Like a sea captain, he swayed back across the room and threw a small parcel at me which I caught more out of a reflex for self-defence than any surprise at the gift, for it came at me like a stone aimed at my balls. 'Happy Christmas, George,' he said in a tone more of menace then felicitation.

'Thank you very much,' I said.

'Well open it,' he said with a sneer.

It was a small gold lighter from Aspreys. 'Thank you,' I said.

'That's all right, George, that's all right,' he said with a little mocking bow. 'You can impress your friends in Paddington.'

And then turned to Maureen. 'And now for you, my lovely. First this.' He handed her a package.

To watch her unwrap it was like watching, and I must apologise for the inevitable simile, because there is nothing more accurate, a child. Her fingers trembled and fumbled as she broke the scotch tape, looking up all the time to confirm his reactions, while her face was fixed in nervous concentration. When she arrived at the thin black case that the paper concealed, she opened it slowly, savouring the suspense, then gasped, shut the box again, smiled, started to cry and threw her arms round his neck, saying, 'Thank you, thank you. It's lovely. It's the most wonderful present I've ever had.'

'Well let's see it on, for Christ's sake,' he said.

At which she sniffed and picked up the case, opened it and brought out a thin thread of platinum suspended from which was a small cross of diamonds and emeralds. She placed it round her neck and tried to fix the clasp, but her fingers were too nervous and excited and she pleaded, 'Help me, I can't do it,' and he replied, 'George will do it for you.'

I marvelled at this man who could be so extravagantly generous and yet so incapable of acknowledging it. It was as if he could only deal with altruistic feelings, which clearly embarrassed him, by countering with an aggressive offhand manner. I went round to Maureen and joined the clasp.

'How does it look?' she said, and gave an elegant curtsy and then 'I want to see how I look,' and dashed off to find a mirror.

In her absence he poured himself another drink and lit a cigar, yet there was something in his manner which implied unfinished business, and in this brief interval he was savouring its anticipated completion. His lips held the cigar in a kind of smirk and I had a feeling, which proved to be so sadly correct, that the forthcoming action would centre on and emanate from the long thin flat parcel that still lay, unopened before him.

She returned joyously, flushed with her own self-love and admiration. Her query, 'You don't think my neck's too thick?' was merely a ruse to draw as many reassurances and compliments as possible her way, but her man was not to be drawn. Instead he picked up the last parcel and held it out at her.

'What's this?' she said.

'Another present for you,' he said.

There was something sinister and chilling in the way he said it that made her hesitate and look anxiously at him. She glanced over at me as if I might offer any explanations or clues, but I could only shrug my ignorance amiably back at her.

'It's not a bomb,' he said impatiently. 'Open it for Christsake.'

She undid the parcel in a tentative way, knowing that its contents could only be an anticlimax to her beautiful pendant, but she knew from the way that he was looking at her, leaning forward in anticipation, stroking his chin, that he was eager for her to comply. She looked down into the litter of wrapping paper at a large cardboard box whose contents she seemed puzzled by. Recognition made her blush a bright red.

'Well let's see them, then,' he said.

'It's silly,' she said defensively, 'I'm embarrassed.'

'Let's see them,' he insisted.

She held up a pair of nylon briefs, in a transparent rosy red, from the legs of which hung thin, long black suspenders. The crotch was decked with a small brush of artificial black pubic hair. She gave an awkward self-conscious giggle. Together with the briefs was a bra, in matching material and colour, the nipples of which were set by twin silver and sequin buds. They bore the distinctive trade mark of a certain Soho shop renowned to fetishists the world over.

He said, 'Don't you like them?'

And she, still anxious to please, still somewhat frightened by him, still insecure with him, said, 'Well, when would I wear them?'

'Well, right now for a start.'

She coloured again. 'Don't be silly.'

'I'm not being silly,' he said quietly. 'Go and put them on now. I'd like to see you in them. And I'm sure George would too.'

I had been feeling more than uneasy myself throughout their whole exchange, but the mention of my name made me alarmed. When he stared across at me his face had a demonic, set look which I avoided, remaining silent.

'Go and put them on,' he insisted.

'No,' she said, challenging him, at which he got angry and shouted, 'I bought them. I want to see them. Go and put them on.' And there was no let-out in his face. He was in deadly earnest, and she knew this. She looked at him pleadingly as if he might change his mind, but he remained so fixed and determined that she gave in, snatched up the garments and ran upstairs.

He rolled the cigar between finger and thumb. 'Does that sort of thing turn you on, George?'

'I don't know,' I said curtly. 'It's not the sort of thing I go in for.'

'You should do,' he said. 'You don't know what you're missing.'

I confess I found the whole scene distasteful, and I could hardly contain my anger, yet there is something so overpowering in the man which makes me check myself at every turn, and I tried a more rational approach, conciliatory.

'Why Maureen? There are thousands of other girls in the world for that sort of thing. It's obviously not her style.'

'That's the whole point,' he said.

And I have to admit that perhaps it was, for shortly after she came back into the room still modestly wearing a dressing gown, I felt I understood what he was at. She stopped some feet away from the table, her head and eyes lowered, and he beckoned her nearer.

How can I describe an event which had all its roots and rhythms in the subculture of pornography without lapsing into a pastiche of its style? How can I convey also a genuine eroticism without declining into the vulgar and the obvious? It would doubtless need the skill of someone more adept than I, but when David pulled her roughly to him, and lifted aside the veils of her gown and cast it on the floor the spectacle of the superb body of that woman sent juddering shivers through me. She stood there magnificent, soft, sensual, flowing, curving, rounded, tactile, milky, the full line of her hips edged by the almost brazenly comic line of those gauzy drawers, their little artificial bush winking so come hither from her crotch, her thighs striped with the saucy straps of suspenders that tugged at her black-stockinged long and lovely legs, not to mention her soft mounding belly, her deep navel, her waist, her full creamy bosom cupped cheekily in the transparent bra with those two vulgarly glittering nipples, and setting it off in such heartbreaking contrast the chaste cross of diamonds and emeralds at her throat. Such was her body, but the quality that drove a man to distraction, and drove me to a desire that shamed me, was the absolutely modest and self-effacing way she stood there, shy, gawky, nervous, embarrassed and confused. And it was at this point of contradiction, and I realised this in a flash of erotic inspiration, that her attraction lay, and drew him so eagerly to her. The body of a tart and the modesty of a nun.

I write now of course in recollected and more honest tones, free of the awkward shame I felt then for my responses which turned me angrily against him and made me so solicitous of her plight. And he sensed my reaction and as if to provoke me and her the more, pulled her roughly onto the sofa and kissed her extravagantly before my eyes. She was sobbing with tears as much perhaps of passion as of humiliation, I do not know, but I dashed out of the door in savage contempt for him, slamming it behind me, and made for the retreat and refuge of the boat house.

There I stayed, uneasily aroused, trying to distract myself with a book.

His behaviour seemed to me totally inexplicable, so deliberate and as if the whole holiday had been planned with that one episode in mind. Yet what was even more perverse was the public way in which the humiliation was conducted, and I could not help feeling that it was not merely an added sadistic spice, for he could as well have taken such pleasures alone with her in the bedroom where doubtless she would have participated with love and enthusiasm, nor was it a voyeuristic show arranged for his pleasure or for mine. Rather it occurred to me that there was something irrevocable in the act, as if he had pushed events to a point from which no return was possible. It seemed to me a calculated destructiveness on his part, an attempt to so brutalise the affair that it was impossible for either to continue in the same way. Was he perhaps ruthlessly excising her from his life, hoping to destroy any feeling she had for him?

I suppose I lay on the couch thinking, reading in snatches for just over an hour when I heard the car start and drive away. I gave it no more thought and shortly I fell asleep, exhausted and perplexed by the events of the day. When I awoke it was quite dark, and a glance at my watch, which read nine p.m., confirmed that I had been unconscious for several hours. Some second sense made me look over to the window where I saw to my surprise Maureen, staring out at the flashing, repeating light of Fastnet lighthouse. I got up from the couch and she turned to me. 'He's gone,' she said.

'Where?'

'Back to London.'

'That's nice,' I said, then added as an urgent afterthought, 'Well how the hell are we going to get home?'

'He's fixed up with a local driver to take us to the airport tomorrow.'

Well I suppose it was one of those extra little spiced surprises that one could expect from a mystery holiday with Mr Adler. I looked out of the window. At least the mist had lifted but he couldn't have chosen a more remote spot to maroon us. It was seventy odd miles east to the airport and to the west was nothing but the rolling black breakers of the Atlantic with New York some three thousand miles away.

'Well, we're stuck here,' I said and lit a cigarette. 'But it's a bloody imposition. Why did he go?'

'He got moody and depressed and wanted to go.'

'Couldn't we have shared his mood with him at least? And all travelled back together?'

'He said he wanted to be on his own.'

'It's amazing how the mighty are such slaves to their whims.'

'I brought some scotch with me,' she said, showing the bottle. 'Do you want a drink?'

'Why not? There's not much else to do.' She poured out a glass.

'Merry Christmas,' I said.

'He was drunk earlier,' she said for no reason. 'I don't think he really meant to embarrass you.'

'It wasn't me. I would have thought it was more you.'

She sipped her glass like a bad movie star, and shrugged, 'Why should I mind. I love him.'

I might just have managed to conceal a wince. In the silence that followed I began to feel uneasy. The memory of her part-naked just a few hours before was still fresh in my mind, and the truth did occur to me that we were very much alone, and she was in her own particular way desirable. The realisation of this, and the conscious efforts I made to suppress it, succeeded in making me if not irritable at least more impatient and forthright. I felt tired of being merely part of the audience, merely applauding the show, and thought it was time for some critique, some assessment. What on earth did she mean anyway by 'I love him'? I said, 'What the hell's going to happen between you two?'

'That's up to him, I think,' she said.

'But why? You're part of it, you're involved in it. What do you want?'

'I want him,' she said, with an unequivocation which I suppose I could only envy. Certainly in all my life I had never arrived at such certainty.

'But what if he doesn't want you?'

'Then I'll be miserable. But he does want me.'

'Are you sure?' said Job's comforter and then unfairly perhaps, 'What about earlier?'

'That proves that he wants me, doesn't it?' She picked up a large shell from the window sill and scratched her face with it thoughtfully.

'It seemed to me a pretty insensitive thing to do. I know I could never …'

But she cut me off with, 'But you're not a bit like him. That's just his way.' She looked at me quizzically. 'You don't really like him do you?'

And so she put me on the spot. I could have said a lot of things that might have merely added up to a lifetime's resentment, so I settled for, 'Sometimes I think he's a bastard, yes.'

She smiled with an awful kind of knowing wisdom, 'That's because you're not a woman.'

If there's one thing that raises my hackles it's so-called feminine intuition, part of the mystique of womanhood that serves as a palliative to women's own oppression and subservience. It's a piece of voodoo that all oppressed tribes take refuge in. It is the more maddening because there is no answer to it. I nodded a wry affirmative. 'You mean you're prepared to tolerate it.'

She giggled, 'You are funny George. You really are?'

'What do you mean?' I said, unamused.

'You just are.' And that seemed to satisfy her, for she gave no explanation.

'You're not really a film writer, are you?'

I looked at her wondering if she was guessing, and wondering at the same time why I felt some loyalty to him to cover up for his lies. She seemed to know what I was thinking for she added, 'I asked the local projectionist. He's mad about films. He's never heard of you. And he knows every film since they were silent.'

'No I'm not a film writer,' I said.

'He asked you to pretend, didn't he?'

So why should I defend him? 'That's right.'

'You see, that proves he wants me.'

It's a logic that defeats me, a way of thinking that looks only to confirm what it wants to confirm. I got up and put more peat on the fire. She seemed suddenly a lot more shrewd than I had believed her to be. I poked at the ashes for a while.

She said, 'You're not jealous of me, are you?'

I blew out a long exasperated sigh. 'I don't think so.'

'Only friends sometimes are,' she added quickly. I picked up a packet of cigarettes and lit one. 'Maureen,' I said, 'David and I aren't particularly friends. We grew up together but we have little else in common. I live in a small part-furnished flat in Paddington on the dole. I'm a rather defeated person. And rather confused.'

'Well, why do you see him then?'

'He commands my presence,' I said, I hoped ironically. 'And besides it's tough living on the dole.'

This seemed to please her for she came over to me and kissed me on the cheek. 'You're sweet.' she said. 'And a bit cunning too.'

It seemed the final cadenza to that particular part of the conversation, or maybe simply neither of us had more to reveal on the subject. We drank a bit and talked for more than an hour, by which time I began to feel tired and yawned extravagantly.

'I ought to go to bed,' I said.

She got uneasy at this and said, 'I'm frightened to sleep alone in that house. I'm not used to it. Can I sleep here? With you?'

There was that terrible moment of hesitation as a number of desires stirred themselves, and she was not totally unaware of them, for she added, 'Just as friends. Nothing else.'

I undressed in the sheepish way that 'friends' do. Shoes first, then shirt, then trousers, sitting on the end of the bed, and in my Y-fronts leapt manfully between the icy sheets. Of course I had given furtive glances in her direction, wondering how much she would divest herself of, but she settled to sleep in her slip, bra and pants. Whether she was still wearing her Christmas underwear I never found out. I switched off the light, preferring the anonymity of the dark, as she slipped between the sheets.

I lay there stiffly for a while, feeling the heat from her body radiate towards me. She was lying on her back, staring at the ceiling. Suddenly she turned to me and kissed me on the cheek. 'You're very sweet,' she said, before turning her back on me, her arse warmly on my belly.

I spent the night in a state of restless erection, listening to her breathing, the occasional grinding of her teeth. Little irregular gasps, and once she turned over still sleeping, her arms around me. I often wonder why I didn't screw her. I wanted to more than anything. I certainly might have slept better. But I didn't and perhaps it says something against me, and explains a little what and why I am – George, the regular gent. Anyway the dawn came up, and I watched her shadowy face getting clearer and more defined in the developing day, and saw to my surprise that contentedly and noisily she was sucking her thumb.

Chapter 12

For three months now I had been involved, sporadically but I felt to some extent crucially, in their relationship, but my role in it still remained something of a mystery, primarily because I was dealing first and foremost with a man whose inner motives and feelings are elusive, seldom revealed, held down within himself, and even though at times it seemed to me that he was on the brink of a revelation, as if he had been hesitating for some time to take me genuinely into his confidence and talk, at the decisive point he drew back. Something was bothering him, that I knew, but what it was I could only guess. His uncertainty centred on his feelings for Maureen, an insecurity that pulled him this way and that. He was in the grip of some emotion that affected him profoundly, yet disturbed him at the same time. He did not like the implications of his attraction for her and in Ireland maybe he had tried to destroy it, but the outcome of that particular exhibition was not possibly what he had intended, or maybe it was calculated and played out exactly as he had contrived it. Both are possible and it says something about the ambiguous nature of his own personality.

At all events their relationship took a different turn. In London he began appearing with her in public, taking her to theatres and clubs, and I imagine this must have made her more than happy. She came to London more frequently, staying nights.

How Ted reacted to this I was not immediately certain, but there must have been some kind of confrontation between husband and wife. Either those brief occasions when they now saw each other were dominated by tension and resentment, or else he had capitulated for his own reasons to her demands. On the times when I saw her I could only marvel at how ruthlessly she could dismiss him from her thoughts and actions. She seldom mentioned him.

With the more public turn in David and Maureen's relationship, the significance of my role waned somewhat. Occasionally I would get a call or request from him to entertain her while he was busy, and sometimes I took her to dinner or the cinema before returning her to him at his flat. He always paid me handsomely for these small favours, covering my expenses so excessively that I came away the richer by some twenty or thirty pounds. I won't pretend that I was not often inconvenienced or actually put out by his requests, but inevitably I complied, and the more cynical reader may guess, perhaps rightly, that the reimbursement was often more than a compensation.

In truth I began to find her company dull. It might simply be that familiarity dulled my response to her, but this is not entirely the case for I sensed a certain change in her. She seemed to me no longer the pathetically sad young woman from the provinces whom life had treated so offhandedly. Perhaps it says more of my own fantasy structure to state a preference, but her earlier uncertainty and timidity had a pathos that made her appealing, in a way that certainly her new-found confidence, brashness almost, did not.

Somehow she became merely vulgar. The original despairing yearning for a dream had a poignancy, whereas its realisation highlighted merely the brittle empty tinsel of its content. The new clothes that he lavished on her made her a wealthy commonplace, along with the jewels and ornaments. Her conversation was full of, to me, boring accounts of clubs she had been to and people she had met, catalogues of names boasted about, gossip announced with a familiarity that I found the more irritating because it concerned relationships so recently made. When she announced that she was to enter the London Clinic at his expense to have her nose altered by plastic surgery it seemed to me that our conversation was complete. I looked forward merely now to counting up the ill-gotten gains of my expense account.

Of course I offer merely opinions and impressions. Some might say that I describe them in too perfunctory a way, that I skim over the profound psychological shifts and motives of the young woman's soul and its development. True enough

– a fault that runs no doubt like a fissure in a rock face throughout this whole narrative. But I am not without prejudice, neither am I the omniscient presence of the Victorian novelist, breathing life into his literary canvas with all the purposeful and moral imperatives of that age. I give merely an account of a series of events that took place in our time. Speculations I offer, but omniscience I do not have. I do not control the lives of the characters I write of.

I do not pretend to have in my power some life and motive diviner. I do not know the inner psychological motives, the inner feelings of my characters. I know only what they reveal outwardly. What I do know are the events that took place, the contradictions and conflicts that arose out of these events. I recount them because they might seem to have a significance, they might be a personalised record of a certain way of living in this year of 1972. That is my sole purpose. To recreate to the best of my albeit limited ability the feel, the physical quality, the outlines of a personality, the salient points of action, the mythology, the aspirations, the illusions, the fantasies, and the brutal outcome of their realisation.

My vision is of course limited, subjective, inasmuch as my own personal tastes and preoccupations colour my reactions. If so far in this account, and I insist on the word, I have focused the attention of the reader upon the dramatis personae as seen by one who directly participated in the opening mechanism of the events, it was in order to communicate a certain flavour, a certain personal response. But the events that followed found me more or less an observer on the sidelines rather than an active participant: I merely witnessed the hints, remarks, indiscretions, sundry details out of which I have built the total picture that I now present.

What follows was well beyond my control and represents the inexorable clash of interests that a certain system provokes in so inevitable a way. That it is a mode of operation so fraught with contradiction I merely draw your attention to; that it is a mode of operation that takes place daily in the confusing welter of exchange and production of commodities whose sole end is the extraction of profit, I only remind you of. And it is not so much a tragedy of our times that I relate, but merely the casual hazards of our organisation of resources. It is this that dominates all other intentions.

So, as I said, I retreat to the sidelines, more guide than actor. The action shifts elsewhere.

He, our hero, David Adler, returned from Ireland and whatever else was on his mind when he left so impulsively was rapidly ousted by an irritating piece of business news. Arrangements for the purchase of the expiring leases in the town of his birth had gone satisfactorily. Every shopkeeper had listened to the persuasive explanations of the young company spokesman who had been delegated the task, and his offers of handsome compensation and, moreover, promises of profitable and up-to-date sites in the future provided no meagre incentive. Enthusiasm would best describe the way these small but ambitious merchants, who had struggled all their lives in the dim perspective of the dark and obsolete premises where they had stored and distributed their merchandise of hardware, bicycles, radios and radiograms, drugs, vegetables, wines and spirits, sportswear and school uniforms, grasped their pens and affixed their signatures in blue black ink.

All, that is, but one: one who had shown greater initiative in the past, greater ambition, perhaps greater imagination, one who had developed the small modest grocery business that he had inherited from like-minded parents into a thriving, expanded and redesigned modern emporium that employed all of three cashiers and five stockers and had a turnover high enough to ensure most of his modest demands. There are no surprises, neither do I intend to build up suspense, so I now tell you that the name of the store was Hardin's, and its owner none other than Ted.

Sentimentalists will see his reluctance, indeed his refusal, to sign away his lease in favour of another more powerful enterprise as the revenge of a slighted lover, but this was not the case. At that stage, and security had been jealously guarded by not only Ajax Developments itself but also the worthies of the Town Council and the planning department, Ted was ignorant of the identity of the brain, the power, behind the scheme. In no way did he connect the name of David Adler with Ajax Developments, and why should he have? Even if he had known, his wife's infidelity would undoubtedly have appeared as only a secondary consideration, merely adding the grit of determination to struggle on. From the beginning he was outraged by the suggestion that he should hand over, for whatever sum, all that he had struggled to build up. He dismissed the initial overtures with the indifference and mocking contempt that they deserved. When he closed the door firmly but politely behind the young man who for all his airs and fluency and natty outfit seemed a mere juvenile in dealing with one whose life had been steeled by the rigours of the shop counter, Ted believed that it was the end of a ludicrous presumption. It was to his horror that he discovered that his fellow tradesmen, friends for most of his life, solid, reliable, judicious men, had indicated a willingness to concede to these impudent requests. Already they were speculating on the potential investment of the new capital that was to come their way. He argued with them, ridiculed their intentions, but to his surprise and dismay they seemed resolute and fixed in their determination to go ahead with the suggested proposals. Some seemed almost relieved to be rid of the responsibility that ownership entailed. He left the meeting of the trading association with a profound sense of their treachery and his own isolation, yet with a renewed incentive to fight. When the young man called a second time he was less polite, openly showed his hostility, and told him to go to the devil. 'You'll have to forcibly evict me,' he declared. 'There's not enough money in the Bank of England to make me give up my shop.'

All this was duly recounted to David shortly after Christmas. He listened with a certain amount of irritation and exasperation – there was always one dog in the manger, it was to be expected – before saying, 'All right, offer him a better price. That's what he's after. But don't go mad.'

But in a later encounter with the representative Ted made it only too clear that he was interested in neither the money nor a new site. What did he need a site for when already Hardin's occupied pride of place in the high street, had been renovated to look like new and was doing a brisk and regular trade? He told him a second time to go to hell. There were some things that money could not buy.

Ted's militancy only hid a deep anxiety, however. He began to suffer from feelings of his own isolation, for he lacked allies and there was no one he could turn to. He had long since given up discussing business matters with Maureen for he knew they bored her, and furthermore he knew she had other things on her mind. He was fully aware that she was having an affair with David Adler and he did not mind. Perhaps he suffered some deeply concealed wound, but this he overlaid with altruistic feelings for Maureen's own happiness. For years he had known that he could never make her happy and he had even withdrawn from the task with the kind of acceptance that is only possible for people who have lived many years together. He was contented enough that she should still want to stay with him. He suspected that he had little of the glamour and allure that she so obviously cried out for in the deepest part of her soul, and he was in fact pleased that she had at long last met someone who could satisfy her longings. That a man of such influence as David Adler should take an interest in her seemed somehow to increase her value in his eyes. In short, he derived a certain amount of pleasure from Adler's attention to her, which confirmed the rightness of his choice ten years before.

Therefore to ask David for advice did not seem to him presumptuous. David could be considered in however curious a sense a friend of the family. Ted had never evinced the slightest hostility towards him and had always been warm and solicitous in his company.

Assessing the relationship in this way, he did not hesitate to pen a letter asking whether they might meet up in town at David's convenience, for there was a matter of concern that he wanted to discuss. He posted the letter and anxiously waited a reply from one who was an undisputed expert on such problems. He began to feel more optimistic, as though he had already found an ally.

The letter disturbed David, who anticipated some heated discussion about Ted's piddling property or some jealous demand about his wife. He wondered whether perhaps he should inform Maureen or at least ascertain her husband's mood in advance, but eventually he decided not to. David was not one to avoid confrontations, rather he owed his position to dealing with them to his own advantage. In fact he enjoyed them. He sent a reply to Ted suggesting a time at his, David's, flat. The acceptance came by return of post.

David ushered him formally into the apartment and was surprised by the warm and affirmative way that his assumed adversary shook his hand. He was agitated, obviously with a problem on his mind, but either he was concealing his hostility or it was aimed elsewhere. David offered him a drink and they sat down.

Ted began apologetically, hoping that he was not taking up too much of David's time, and that he would be forgiven for any inconvenience that he had caused. At length, after a hesitating preamble, he got to the core of his concern, which he released with all the force of a pent-up passion. It was the plea of a disturbed and worried man who was desperate for advice.

David listened with a kind of amazement. Never had he anticipated this. The irony was too grotesque. He wondered how he could deal with it. He was tempted not to reveal his identity or role in the drama at first, and wondered whether he could, as it were anonymously, persuade his suppliant to a course of action that would be directly to his advantage. But even one who saw the imperative for scruples in business matters only when they were unequivocally profitable nevertheless felt that he could not conduct the proceedings in this way. There was, moreover, the risk that when Ted discovered his identity, as he inevitably would, he would merely become even more firmly entrenched in his intransigent position. Therefore when Ted finished and looked eagerly into his face for the so keenly sought-after advice, he drew slowly on his cigar, stood up and said:

'Ted, I've got to be absolutely straight with you. You're a businessman and you understand what it's about.'

From one like David Adler that was praise indeed. Ted flashed him a modest smile. He continued:

'I think you've come to me with some misunderstanding. I'm afraid I can't really help you because I'm involved in the city centre development myself.'

Ted's eyes narrowed with incomprehension. He flicked his tongue over his lips. 'I don't understand. What do you mean?'

'I mean,' said David, looking him unflinchingly in the eye, 'that the company of which I'm chairman is currently acquiring all the leases of the centre of Trowbridge in order to develop the site. We've acquired every lease, Ted, except yours.'

These few words produced in Ted Hardin a whole range of confused and conflicting feelings. If he had heard correctly, then it meant that the whole world was turning on an axis of treachery. Here was a man whom he had been happy to consider a friend announcing his intention to remove him of all he possessed, and announcing it in such a cool unruffled tone. Yes, he had heard right and here was he in the very apartment of the person who had now revealed himself as his number one enemy. The realisation made him feel slightly foolish. He felt he should get to his feet and leave without further discussion, but the news had stunned him and his own acknowledged stupidity paralysed him. He gave a short bitter laugh, 'I have come to the wrong place all right,' he said.

David shook his head, 'No I'm glad you've come because we can talk about it man to man in the open. There's nothing sinister in our motives. We want to acquire your lease, that's all, and we want to do it in conditions that are favourable to both of us. That's a fair price to you and probably the offer of a new site when the development is finished. It's a simple business transaction. There are no bad feelings to it.' But Ted had heard it all before and it seemed merely a parody on the lips of David Adler. They could not seem to get it into their heads that he wanted his shop and that was all. There was nothing else to discuss. He said stubbornly, 'I don't want to sell.'

'Look, Ted, I know as well as the next man that people get attached to places. But progress involves change, destroying a bit of the past to make the future better. That's what we're doing, not only for tradesmen but for the whole town.' He was pleased with his reasoning, delivered just with a tremulous edge of conviction. He heard himself continue, 'Let me tell you what the plans are.'

But Ted shook his head, his ears closed. Yet David persisted, 'It'll transform the town. Everyone wants it. There'll be a large modern office block, a whole shopping precinct, covered, no traffic, safe for the kids. And a brand new theatre that I'm donating to the town. I don't think I could be fairer.

Do you want to stand in the way of that, Ted? Because that's what you're doing. You can't hold back progress.' He emphasised the word progress, then picked up his glass and sipped, pleased with his little oration, the more so because it had affected his man, made him hesitate. He could see that Ted had not considered these arguments before, and he thought irritably to himself, 'What the hell do I pay people for, if they can't present the company's case simply and convincingly?' He made a mental note to reprimand his junior executive.

And indeed Ted was given cause to think. He flinched from the reasoned words that accused him at every phrase, that heaped upon him injury and guilt, that tried and judged him before history itself. But then another voice spoke inside Ted's head and it seemed to say with all the experience and cunning that a life in trade had given him, 'That's just PR, the salesman talking, the rep. He wants to persuade me for his own advantage. He's only really concerned with what's in it for him.' And he looked around the plush apartment that was like one opulent symbol of all David's former deals, and in a flash of insight he saw it enriched, more extravagant, at some future date, financed by his own, Ted's, lifeblood. And it was this voice that decided Ted and gave him a new-found eloquence, and he said, 'You can't blackmail me like that. I've got my rights. That shop is mine and I'm going to keep it. You can go to hell.'

Patience comes in limited quantities and David's had reached its limit. Why should he waste any more time? He

147

said flatly, 'Ted, we've invested a great deal of capital in this project and if you think you can hold us to ransom you've got another think coming. We're going ahead with that development, whatever you want. We've tried to be fair, but you refuse to listen. I'm giving you one more chance. You're up against a tough crowd here. You won't find us sentimental. We're a big, influential company. We can break you like a twig.' And he snapped his fingers to illustrate.

'Then you'll have to break me,' said Ted, getting to his feet and heading for the door defiantly.

'Why don't you be reasonable?' The request hung like a terrible temptation in the air. It was offered as a last chance, and Ted paused, half wanting to accept, to be returned to the warmth, to his friends, to a life that was free of pain and struggle and loneliness, but something else drove him on and he turned and said, 'There's nothing else to discuss,' and was gone through the door.

Chapter 13

From that point David determined to destroy Ted with all the means at his disposal.

Hitherto he had borne him no ill-feeling or malice. He had taken Maureen away from him with no special competitive motive, if only because it had never entered his head to consider Ted even remotely worthy of the status of rival. He felt a certain mild contempt for the weaker man, but no more than most adulterers feel for the wronged husband, and he dismissed with a shrug any sense of guilt that others might have felt. In this world he considered that women and others' wives were there to be taken, so they were. That seemed to be an irrefutable statistic, and the suggestion that he had seduced or exerted pressure in some way he found merely laughable. Women had minds of their own and if they preferred him then that was hard luck on the other man. Had their decision gone against him he would have shrugged his shoulders and looked elsewhere.

But now the situation had changed. The weaker man had

deliberately tried to cross him and was standing stupidly and perversely in his way. It wasn't that Ted was any more foolish than most, or that David now viewed him with a passionate and consuming hatred. He merely had to be removed as a stubborn obstacle in his path. It was no mere coincidence either, I imagine, that David then suggested that Maureen should leave Ted and come to live with him.

Maureen was delighted. She was convinced that she had now got her man and that life would reveal all its riches and magic to her. It was almost in an offhand way that she announced her intention to Ted. No one who has lived such unrealised fantasies for that number of years, who found reality a hostile and contradictory shadow cast across her inner desires, can sustain such illusions without being totally self-obsessed, and like most self-obsessed people she showed a marked insensitivity to the needs of others.

In her dealing with Ted therefore, which had of late been perfunctory to say the least, she was casual to the point of cruelty. Admittedly her life with him had not been a whirl-wind of excitement, and I would be the last person to defend him on this score, but I do not feel this gave her licence to discard him like a soiled piece of underwear, which is what she did. She merely packed her case one morning and left him a hasty note. It read, 'Dear Ted, you know how hopeless I am at writing things down, but I hope you will forgive me because I can't say this to your face. I'll always remember you as a kind and considerate man who has worked hard to give me everything I need, but you know by now what I am like, what a dreamer I am and what I feel about David. I can't go on living two lives and now that he wants me to live with him I must go. I don't really know what more to say except that I hope you'll be happy and thank you for all the good times we had together. Love, Maureen.'

He read the note half anticipating its contents, and as he read, rather than causing any sense of loss, it merely confirmed his hatred of David and made him all the more resolved to defy him. He sat back in his chair for a while, staring into the flickering television screen. Then he got up, gathered in his arms all her clothes and possessions that she had been unable to take, and burned them in a paraffin-soaked heap on the front lawn.

He took a certain comfort in the flames that engulfed her discarded garments. In his own dull way he had loved her and had worked for her, but he had never been able to fathom her. Perhaps she was just cheap after all, he thought, a bricklayer's daughter who had never grasped the practical demands that life placed upon the petite bourgeoisie, that much maligned section of the population. But like the ashes now in front of him, she was a thing of the past. His future held a crusade, a fight for the rights of the small shopkeeper against the encroachment of big and unscrupulous business concerns. He warmed to his task, to its challenge, to all the principles involved. Life was changing, freedom was threatened, hostile battalions encircled him, on the one hand a mass of organised workers in their millions demanding their higher wages, their houses, their holidays abroad with no respect for an older tradition of order and dignity and self-help, and on the other the voracious, powerful giants, who were now trying to break him – and the memory of Adler's threat came back to him – like a twig. Perhaps he stood alone, but fight them he would. He returned to the house and switching off all the lights, sat in the darkness, pondering till dawn came.

So Maureen moved in with David and he waited for Ted to change his mind.

I was invited round several days afterwards to celebrate her arrival. They were in the middle of dressing when I walked through the open door, and there was an air of festivity in the penthouse, as though celebrations were still going on. I could see her making herself up in the bedroom, a champagne glass in her hand. The apartment now looked lived in, like a centre from which activity emanated, a change from the somewhat formal temporary quality it had had before. She was bubbling with high spirits and champagne, while he, stripped to the waist, slapped me on the shoulder and offered me a drink.

'Well? You surprised?' he said, grinning.

'I suppose so. Yes,' I said.

'Not as surprised as Maureen was, I can tell you.'

'You can say that again,' she said from the bedroom.

He said, 'I thought we might go out and celebrate. Go to a club or something. What do you say?'

I said it sounded fine.

'Well cheer up then,' he said. 'I'm paying.' And with a laugh he went into the bedroom. He kissed her on the back of the neck and began putting on a shirt.

'George!' she called. 'Can you zip me up?'

I noticed that her hair had been restyled and there were little curlicues around her ears. The top was lacquered and she must have been wearing a hair-piece which dangled down her neck in tiny ringlets. Her make-up was more striking too, especially round the eyes which were set in a green shadow. She looked more poised but harder.

'I've spent nearly all day at the beauty parlour,' she said. 'What do you think of your small town girl?'

'Terrific,' I said, but I couldn't have sounded that convincing for she replied, 'Well you'll have to get used to it, because that's the way I aim to be.'

It was the first time I had seen her since Ireland, and there was something ominous in the remark. It was the first hint I'd had of the beginnings of a change in her and she sensed my apprehension, for almost as if to reproach herself she wrinkled her face and said, 'Does that sound big-headed?'

'I liked you as you were, that's all. And I suppose I'll like you the way you want to be.'

'You are sweet, George,' she said and kissed me on the cheek.

153

'Come on you two,' he said, 'I'm hungry.' He was ready, in dinner jacket and shirt, and a velvet bow tie.

We drove by taxi to a place whose name and location I was not able to ascertain. The cab pulled up in a side street, before the glass doors of what I took at first to be an apartment block. A doorman, dressed in the clothes of a functionary of the turf, opened our door for us, and ushered us to the entrance under cover of a large umbrella, for there was a fine drizzle in the air. For this modest assistance he received from our impresario host the sum of one pound, which he put swiftly into a back pocket, winking his gratitude.

Once through the glass doors we began to climb some carpeted stairs, whose decor somehow reminded me of a large luxury sea liner, for there were small display alcoves, like miniature shop windows, advertising perfumes and watches. On his way down the stairs came a man of striking appearance, with a ruddy lined face and long silver hair that still bore stains, as it were, of its earlier ginger colouring. His shoulders had a certain furtive stoop, and in the same secretive manner he kept his eyes and head down. He moved silently on rubber-soled shoes, the toes turned outwards at forty-five degrees. As he passed us he muttered in a broad cockney accent, 'There's more villainy and form up there than in the whole of Dartmoor.' And he disappeared through the exit below.

The stairs finally debouched onto an enormous hall, the right part of which was roped off as a large restaurant where several hundred people were eating. The left half, however, and it was here I imagined that the real business of the establishment was conducted, was given over to gaming tables, roulette, blackjack and craps. This half was considerably more populated than its twin. The decibel level that greeted my ear was little above a buzz, remarkable for an area of such size and activity.

We were greeted warmly and intimately by a waiter – 'Mr Adler, nice to see you' – and ushered in and out of the tables, with many heads turning, to our own. The first thing I noticed our host do was thrust a five pound note into the waiter's hand, with the generous admonishment, 'See you look after us.' Through a gauze window London's traffic rolled.

I don't remember the food very well but I imagine it was of a reasonably high standard, for my interest, as you might well imagine, was divided between my host and hostess and the assembled throng of voracious gamblers that I could observe only too clearly from the vantage point of my seat.

As for Maureen, she sat there, grandly is the word that springs to mind, or rather her idea of grandeur. She was both excited and tense. Socially she felt awkward, for she could not but be aware that the attention of the room was focused on our table, yet in spite of her unease, which really showed only in the way she moved her legs under the table (throughout the meal her legs were under the seat resting on her toes), the performer in her could not help responding to the audience. She moved her hands a great deal when she spoke, she smiled at waiters, and to my embarrassment, she sent back one course. She drew of course great confidence from him, for at the very outset, when we first sat down, he took her hand and squeezed it reassuringly. Knowing he was there to support her, her confidence mounted. She drank a good deal and laughed a lot, while I felt less and less easy.

It was difficult to know whether inwardly David felt the same irritation, for he must have noticed her manner, even the least observant of spectators could not fail to do so, but there was an indulgence in him that I had not seen before, a certain protectiveness. He reminded me rather of the mythical good son taking his mother out to dine, so solicitous was he of her welfare. He was full of surprises.

As for the other assembled loiterers and chancers, whom we were to join when the meal was concluded, I can only say that I have seldom seen in such concentrated proximity so many blue-rinsed hair-dos, so much décolletage, so much satin and silk, so many rings and jewels, so many dark blue suits and so much feverish greed. From the waiter we received the information that a junket was in for the evening, by which he meant that some one hundred and fifty gamblers and their wives had flown over from California in a chartered Boeing jet to play the tables for the evening, an apparently not uncommon occurrence there. They shared the company of politicians of both sides of the house, businessmen, brokers, journalists, corrupt Middle Eastern sheiks, one who wrote out before my eyes a cheque to the value of forty thousand pounds to meet the evening's losses, speculators on both sides of the law, well-known sporting personalities, and criminals whose form alone on that occasion totalled a good thousand years between them.

At one point during the meal we were greeted by an acquaintance of David's. He wore a dark blue suit, wide at the shoulders, with one button that just held the mohair in place across the barrel chest that he seemed to be constantly expanding, like a weightlifter in a contest. His shirt was starched and white, and hanging from his substantial neck was a thin tie, held in the tightest and smallest of Windsor knots. His shoes were black and polished. His hair was short and Brylcreemed and his face was a smoothly shaven mounting for two of the darkest and narrowest eyes I had ever had assess me. He stood stiffly, legs apart, and bowed only from the waist as he shook our hands. As he gave even this most economical of movements, the scent of Old Spice assaulted my nostrils. His hands, which were large, though soft and manicured, sported a large golden ring from which a diamond flashed. Introductions over (he was pleased to meet Maureen and addressed David as 'me son'), he settled back into his stout legs and shot his cuffs, revealing a gold Longine watch, with a dial face bigger than I had ever seen.

He was sun-tanned, which was explained when he informed us, 'We've just had a lovely cruise down to the Canaries. It was really very nice. I took the old woman and the kids. Plenty of cheap drink, nice quiet, relaxing. Favourite

157

really. They lay everything on you know. Good food, band in the evening. Knowing how dodgy my stomach is, you know, I was a bit worried at first about being sea sick, but no trouble at all. Like glass it was, Dave. Really lovely.' He stood talking in his serious, informative way, a glass of scotch in his right hand, the little finger of which was cocked, rather in the manner of a refined Victorian lady sipping tea.

He concluded, 'Nice to see you, me son. Pleased to meet you,' to Maureen and me, and with a last flick of his cuffs, he rolled off back to his table and friends, notable among whom were a Conservative politician and a progressive bishop.

'Who was that?' asked Maureen.

'I suppose you'd call him a gangster,' said David.

For the tables he pressed into my hand a plastic chip the value of fifty pounds. 'Be lucky,' he said. He gave a similar amount to Maureen. Perhaps some excessive caution held me back from risking my small fortune to the vagaries of the roulette wheel, and it remained stickily in my pocket until I cashed it in on my way out. Maureen displayed no such caution, however, once the rudimentary rules of the game were explained to her. She scattered chips, carré, noir, à cheval, numero with all the abandon possible for one who now knew there was plenty more where it came from, though curiously enough for all the eclecticism of her play she ended the evening with a profit of two hundred and fifty pounds, which is more than can be said of the luckless sheikh whose fate I have described earlier …

Winning brought colour to her cheeks, and she watched the wheel with a concentration and attentiveness that many an academic might envy. She registered her losses with a frown and her gains with a bright smile and shriek. David, on the other hand, seemed uninterested in the exercise, content-ing himself merely to fling a few chips in a rather desultory way onto the green baize. He derived more pleasure from her pleasure, and kept squeezing her hand, saying 'Well done' each time her number came up.

For all the diamonds of vulgar opulence and the copious sprays of deodorant and talc, there was nevertheless an odour of anxiety in the air mingling with the flush of gain, and I began to feel the atmosphere oppressive and enervating. There was a man who farted wetly and sourly each time the ball came to its rattling halt. Likewise an old lady of seventy in a black crepe dress, emeralds in her ears and a green eye shade on her brow, emotionlessly working out her system with pencil and paper, a sheen of perspiration on her shoulder. Expressionless girls stood dumbly at the sides of middle-aged men, compliments of some escort agency or other. It seemed to me that all the ingenuity and resourcefulness of man could be put to some better application than primitive chance.

By midnight my feet were aching and my eyes glazed with cigarette smoke, so I was relieved to hear David say, 'Shall we go?' Though there was a pout of disappointment from Maureen who had obviously found a new and absorbing interest in life, he was adamant and he ushered us to the door.

While Maureen peed or powdered in the ladies' room, he said to me, 'George, you know I'm busy during the day and I don't want Maureen to get bored. She doesn't know anybody yet. I'd like you to do me a favour. I'd like you to take her about, entertain her, keep her happy.' I must have looked disturbed but he went on, 'She likes you. You're her friend. I'll put you on the payroll. A oner a week and expenses. I can't be fairer than that.'

At a hundred a week, fairness did not seem in doubt. Perhaps a more principled or less eroded man might have refused, but since I had the feeling that Maureen might well force her company upon me in any case, it did not seem too reprehensible to get paid for it, so I readily assented.

She issued from the ladies, her new fur coat across her shoulders, happier than she had ever been. And as we got into separate taxis and drove our respective ways we brought to a close the celebration of her elevation into 'the good life'.

She called me the very next day and for the following two weeks we shared her period of primitive accumulation. With her own newly donated bank account she purchased a vast quantity of clothes, jewellery, a Mini Minor, a dog and a leopardskin coat. I waited around in I don't know how many shops, hairdressers, beauty salons, and poodle parlours for the dog. We saw every film in the West End and several musical plays. Twice we attended the ballet, which is the nearest thing I can think of to hell. But for all my boredom, and it came in considerable quantity, there was always the comforting balm of the weekly wage cheque. At the end of two weeks she entered the London Clinic for a nose job, and I, duly solicitous, sat in her small bedroom with her, surrounded by flowers, the television constantly on, champagne in the ice bucket. Looking down into her slightly bruised face with the plaster concealing her new and diminished nose, I thought, 'Maureen Hardin, you have certainly come a long way.'

Whether David had timed her entry into the clinic according to plan I do not know, but her absence made it convenient for him to renew his acquaintance on a rather more informal level with the town planner of Trowbridge Spa.

Alec Bromley, the town planner, was surprised and flattered to receive an invitation to dine in London with David Adler. They had met of course over business discussions, but to meet with him socially was a privilege indeed, especially for one who of late, due to the pressure of work and the demands of his wife and family, had seldom had the opportunity for social intercourse. He was now in his late fifties, a solid man, balding and with glasses that gave him an owlish appearance. He dressed as neatly as he could but again the financial demands made upon him by his wife and two daughters, both of whom were attending small but expensive private schools, were an undeniable strain on his modest salary which, at just over two thousand a year, seemed to him insufficient for one who occupied so important a position in council work.

It had been a struggle for Alec all his life. He had had few parental advantages, and had slogged his way through night school to qualify as a chartered surveyor. By nature he was serious, as many self-educated men are, a great reader but inclined to be somewhat pompous in his opinions and boring with it. He had acquaintances rather than friends and had reached that time of his life when he was beginning to wonder whether all his efforts had really been worthwhile. Life certainly seemed considerably easier for the young of today than he had known it, and he could not help feeling a certain resentment towards, for example, his younger assistants, who had had all the advantages of a university education and seemed to take so much for granted.

They lacked a sense of public responsibility, of dedication, the kind that had sent him into local government and housing. But behind this resentment there was a certain uneasiness within him that made him question whether his choice of career had been as adventurous as it could have been. Public service was not something to be ashamed of but he knew that intermingled with it was a kind of timidity, a craving for security, that in the past had held him back from riskier enterprises that might have been more lucrative. Certainly several of the former colleagues he had trained with had been extremely successful in property speculation. Others of course had refused the great demands made on them and were now in a much worse position than he himself was. There were compensations for security, the more so as he was getting older, but nevertheless the doubts remained and nagged him. And not least among these doubts was age itself. Retirement was not that far off, seven years perhaps, and there was always that constant anxiety that he might be replaced by a younger man. It would be hard to fault the way he carried out his job, for he was a methodical, meticulous worker, and he took a certain comfort in that, but all the same the fear remained.

Materially too he'd derived modest gains. His house was comfortable but not overlarge and the mortgage repayments would not be completed for another five years. He had improved the property, he felt, beyond recognition, with central heating, an extended kitchen and lounge, but all these improvements he had had to do with his own hands at weekends.

His car which was now three years old was a Morris 1100, in excellent condition for he lavished much attention and wax on its paintwork, and saw that it was regularly serviced, but nevertheless he felt a certain humilation as he parked it in the Town Hall Car Park, that several of his juniors sported racier, newer models.

Social life too was limited. He enjoyed the cinema which he attended regularly once a week with Audrey his wife. Together they also attended certain functions such as dances, the occasional dinner. Each year they motored to the Dordogne and enjoyed the local wines, sleeping in a large comfortable tent that had seen service now for five summers.

He loved the Dordogne, its valleys and rivers, musky evenings, the smells of the earth. He could think of no more perfect ambition than to retire and end his days there with Audrey in a small farmhouse. He sighed as he thought of it, for even at fifty-seven it seemed a remote possibility and, thus thwarted, a certain bitterness about his life made him restless and resentful.

Even this sketchy outline of a life can explain the excitement and sense of occasion that the invitation from David had produced. Audrey was delighted for him, and they spent a whole evening discussing it, arguing about what he should wear, whether the occasion demanded a new suit or new tie. He laughed at her enthusiasm and rejected any extravagance. All the same, she sent his suit to the express cleaners and bought him a new tie, charging it to their budget account at the local large store. He looked, she felt, most presentable in his dark grey double-breasted suit, a white shirt and the new, daring spotted red tie. He protested as she gave his coat yet another going over with the clothes brush, but she knew that he was excited and she was happy for him.

The chauffeur-driven Rolls Royce pulled up at the house, with the compliments of its young owner, David Adler, and he was ushered into the back like a celebrity. As he sped towards London, he felt this was the only way to travel.

David waited for him in the bar of Carlton Towers, and shook his hand warmly. Alec was surprised, but agreeably so, that a young woman was present. She was young, with the fairest of hair and the bluest of eyes. She wore a skirt that barely covered her, and when she sat down she displayed the longest and shapeliest legs he had ever seen. Her skin was clear, her perfume clean. She reminded him of the kind of girl that he saw in advertisements in his teenage daughters' magazines. He thought with more than a little envy that this was the kind of girl that David Adler had.

They had several drinks at the bar and the whisky warmed Alec's stomach and loosened his mind. Young Adler was certainly entertaining and his girl delightful.

When they went to eat he was thrilled that the girl sat next to him and that she paid him so much attention throughout the meal. She seemed so interested in him, asking questions about his life, and though he answered shyly and self-deprecatingly, convinced that whatever he had to say could be of little interest to her, at home in such opulent and exciting surroundings, but far from discouraging her this made her all the more attentive. Once she reprimanded him, lightly and jokingly of course, for his modesty. He chuckled his apologies back.

It must have been during dessert, when he was full of the best of food and the finest of wines, that he felt her leg brush against him. Almost instantly he withdrew, thinking it some clumsiness on his part that the wine had induced, but a moment later it was back again, and this time he was bold. He left his knee there and could feel the warmth of her young leg through his trousers. He was not sure if it was his imagination, but it seemed that she was pressing against him more firmly and he answered by returning the pressure.

He felt confused at first when she stood up at the end of the meal and excused herself, wondering if perhaps he had driven her away by his importunity. He felt a dull flush burn his face and for a second felt wretched. He watched her walk between the tables, so young and racy and carefree. There was something jaunty and defiant in her shoulders and the way she flicked her long fair hair as she moved.

Young Adler said, 'She's a nice girl, isn't she?' and Alec heard himself reply almost too emphatically, 'Utterly charming.'

Brandies arrived and cigars. Adler said, 'I don't want to bore you with business, but we've hit a bit of a snag with the project.'

Alec forced himself to look towards David, away from the entrance that he had been watching so vigilantly for her return. 'Snags? What's that? There are no snags as far as we are concerned.'

'We're having trouble with Ted Hardin. He won't dispose of his lease. He's holding up the whole scheme.'

'I've always found him a reasonable enough chap.'

'Well, he's not being reasonable right now. He refuses categorically to part with it.'

Alec scratched the back of his neck. There was something so reassuring in a fat Havana cigar. He blew out the smoke.

'Well, I'm sure we can find a way round that, can't we? You do have our full support.'

'I think maybe there is something you can do. As a council you have powers of compulsory purchase. That's right, isn't it?'

'For our own schemes, yes.'

'Well, in a manner of speaking this is one of your schemes. At least you are endorsing it.'

'Yes, but I don't think it's quite the same thing,' said Alec with a smile. He had slipped back into his committee room manner.

'Why isn't it?' asked David lightly.

'Because we aren't financing it.'

'You mean you're being spared the burden of financing.'

He chortled. 'I suppose you could say that.'

'Then why can't you purchase compulsorily?'

'Well, I'd have to give it some thought.'

'Do.'

But she was making her way back to the table and Alex felt a tremor in his bowels. He stood up to allow her through and she brushed lightly by him like a soft caress. She joined them in a brandy and he was thrilled to find her leg by his as before. Though this time there were even more unexpected heights of pleasure, for she began ever so gently to stroke the inside of his thigh, and scarcely able to endure the rush of desire that ran through him, he took her hand and squeezed it. It felt so cool and dry and slender in his own, so much a contrast to his thick fingers with their crop of fine reddish hair on the knuckles. He hoped she would not find them repellent, too moist and hamlike. He scarcely dared look at her, and puffed at his cigar with his free right hand.

'Shall we go back to my place?' said David.

'It's not too late?' Alec enquired uneasily, sensing that perhaps the whole delicious evening was breaking up. 'To get me back home I mean?' he added.

'The chauffeur will drop you at the door.'

'Will you join us?' he asked her, the fear of loss giving him unexpected courage.

She looked across at David. 'Well perhaps I ought to get home.'

He felt a terrible sinking feeling. 'Oh, please stay,' he said.

'Well, I must make a phone call,' she said.

'Call by later,' said David. 'It's only across the road.'

'OK,' she smiled and squeezed Alec's hand with more than a hint of promise.

Perhaps it was only the waiter, as he pulled away their chairs, who noticed her wink at David Adler.

The flat was even more than he had imagined, and once again he felt that deep pang of longing and resentment at his own humdrum lot. He was flushed from drink and the central heating made him feel so warm that he wanted to unbutton his shirt collar. Adler placed an even larger brandy in his hand. He looked up into his grey-green eyes. 'It's been a most enjoyable evening,' he said. 'Most enjoyable. You've been very generous.'

'You won't find me an ungenerous person,' said David with a smile.

'You certainly have a wonderful flat,' he nodded wistfully and David bowed his thanks. He sat in a chair facing him.

'Life's not easy for you I imagine,' he said. 'Your salary's not exactly enormous, is it?

He felt suddenly defensive. 'It's sufficient.'

'In my experience the last thing that money is is sufficient. You can always do with more.'

'I suppose that's true,' he chuckled.

'You know, Alec,' there was something consoling about the use of his first name, something American, something private, 'you can do me a big favour and if you did you'd find me more than generous.'

'I suppose you mean compulsorily purchase,' he said with a nervous laugh.

The reply was quiet, fur smooth, with a little affirmative nod. 'That's right.'

Alec felt flustered, with an uneasy suspicion that he was about to be bribed. It had never happened to him before. 'Well I can raise it with the committee.'

'Alec, what you say goes. You're the real authority.'

'Yes, but all decisions are democratic.'

'That's balls and you know it.' The sudden obscenity surprised Alec and he gave a little cough. David went on. 'You want this scheme to go through. There's no point in labouring that. And one idiotic man is standing in the way. You have the power.'

'I can only raise it with the committee,' he said, but faltering.

'Alec, I'll give you ten thousand pounds in ten pound notes or any way you want it if you'll agree.'

The sum echoed in his slightly befuddled brain in all its enormity. He wondered if he had heard right. Ten thousand. A cottage in the Dordogne. His mind raced around the possibilities. And before he could even reply, offer some however mild protest, Adler had gone over to a writing desk, pulled out a large brown package and dropped it in his lap.

'It's yours,' he said. 'Just a gesture of my gratitude.'

'But supposing anyone finds out?' he heard himself ask, and was surprised by the commitment it implied.

'Alec, who's to know? There's nothing illegal in a gift. You can have it in dollars, in francs, in a Swiss account, any way you like. Tax free.'

Of a sudden Alec Bromley felt confused to the point of wretchedness. Lying in his lap was a small bundle that could transform his life and he wanted so much to take it into his grasp, to caress it, to say heal me of my pain and my hardship. Yet something reminded him of his position, of his authority, of his previous incorruptibility, even though he had to admit that no one had ever tried to corrupt him before. But as if to answer his gnawing doubts, Adler said, 'Don't be a mug, Alec.

There's no taste in nothing. Get hold of ten grand and enjoy yourself. You've worked hard most of your life, for what? For a toffee apple. Do yourself a favour.'

There was something settled in the way he said it, as if he assumed that Alec's mind was made up and he had agreed. And his words were so soothing, so much what he wanted to hear and so persuasive.

He sat on the sofa, his head buried in his hands, and slightly dizzy from drink, but the bundle was still there, more eloquent than any words. He could feel its promises almost beating in his lap describing the future with all the imagination it could muster and bring. He was unaware of David's departure, so preoccupied was he with the bright new look of his future, and so silent were the other's parting footsteps. Neither did he notice the girl's arrival till he felt her hand ruffling his hair and when he looked up and saw the face that was so young and desirable smiling down at him, bringing echoes of longings that had been so long buried, he gave a strange strangled moan of joy and buried his face in her lap. He watched with a curious but exciting remoteness, as though it were not happening to him, as she dropped down to her knees and, leaning forward with her young and moist lips pursed, unzipped his flies.

Concealed from his sight a camera clicked as if to preserve for all time his moment of ecstasy and as a warning safeguard should he ever change his mind.

Chapter 14

At that stage I was totally ignorant of the drama that was developing and it was none other than Ted who advised me of it. I was spending the evening alone in my flat. It had been relatively peaceful, disturbed only by the occasional thumps and bangs from the tenant upstairs, an insomniac writer who was trying to reverse the pattern of his agony by working by night and sleeping by day. He based the reversal on the assumption that if he had missed an entire night's sleep physical exhaustion would ensure slumber, but alas, his calculations were wrong, and he was soon back on the sodium amytal only this time for the hours of daylight. I mention this at some length not to divert but merely to explain the bangs, which were caused by his unfortunate attempts to regain consciousness and involved him staggering around his room, often crashing dazed and somnolent to the floor. I accepted these occurrences as a matter of course, though I admit that at an earlier period they caused me some alarm and, anxious for his safety, I had dashed above to find him apparently drunk on the floor, blinking in surprise at my unexpected entry. His problem has my deepest sympathy, but I limit contact now to brief exchanges on the landing. I have no idea what he writes.

It was partly to obliterate the noise, but more to indulge in a newly discovered passion, that I was wearing my recently acquired – the gains of a hundred a week – stereo earphones, which sent me into a trance-like and self-absorbed state, wrapped in the protective covers of penetrating orchestral sounds. I had grown addicted to a certain Albinoni organ concerto and I would lie on my back, the soft padded twin speakers in my ears, transported by the mellow tone of the organ. In such a position one is unable to hear even the loudest of noises from the busy street or jumbo-jetted sky, neither the telephone nor the door bell, nor indeed a shouting human voice at a distance of two feet. Imagine my surprise therefore when I turned my face, illuminated as it was by the sensual aural pleasure, and found shouting into mine the distraught features of Ted Hardin. I was indeed startled, and the impact of the shock sent my earphones sliding around my neck, and my ears, rudely snatched from the thrilling concerto, were now assailed by the totally incomphrehensible statement, 'Forgive me for coming in but I thought you were out.' It seemed somewhat excessive lengths to go to avoid my company.

'No I'm in,' I said. 'Listening to the gramophone as a matter of fact.'

'There was no answer when I rang the door bell.'

'No there wouldn't be, because I wouldn't have been able to hear it.'

I got to my feet, driven in part by the macabre nature of our exchange, which I felt I could no longer tolerate from the vantage point of the floor.

'Have a seat,' I offered, and he looked about him willing to oblige, till frustration overtook him, and a puzzled expression clouded his face. I understood his puzzlement, for I do not live in neat surroundings and at that moment a pile of books was concealing the only chair. I have several thousand books stacked in random bundles about the floor, there being only one small bookcase quite inadequate to house them all. Much as I respect literature I do not have a fetishistic attitude to books themselves, and treat them in a firm yet affectionate manner. I merely scooped up the bundle and dropped it onto the floor. He smiled his gratitude and sat down and started to sniff.

'What is it?' he enquired.

'Joss sticks,' I replied, and so it was. They have for me no special spiritual or religious significance, but I find the odour not unpleasant and it does conceal somewhat the otherwise pervasive smell of dust and damp. I could see, however, that Ted was disconcerted by the news. Scarcely had he adjusted to the unfamiliar surroundings, the disorder within, not to mention the blacks without, than he was confronted with the incense of the Orient. He looked around uneasily for evidence of marijuana or, worse, hypodermic syringes. His worst fears were confirmed when I produced a packet of Turkish cigarettes – small luxuries I now permitted myself – and lit one. He sniffed the air again like a Bugs Bunny character and grew nakedly alarmed when I offered him one. He almost knocked the pack out of my hands with his emphatic refusal, and spent the entire duration of our conversation perched on the rim of the chair, poised for rapid flight should the drug squad call with their slavering Alsatian dogs.

His fear might well have given a greater sense of urgency to the story he told me, but I had the impression of a man who was clutching at a last desperate straw. He spoke rapidly, a terrible tremor in his voice, smoking one tipped Senior Service after another, a thing he had not done on the earlier occasions I had encountered him. I think it was only with the utmost self-control that he prevented himself from breaking into tears. His whole body was taut with nervous tension and, at one point, his left leg, which he had rested, so to speak, on his toe, began to shake and quiver in the most alarming fashion. But it was the need to communicate that drove him on, that enabled him to collect his resources and overcome these physical manifestations. Once I had granted him an audience, the words poured out of him.

After Maureen had left him in her casual and self-obsessed way, he heard nothing from David Adler nor his minion, the dapper juvenile he hated so much. He was uncertain of what could happen, but he interpreted their silence as a retreat from an initiative, and each day as he waited anxiously for the mail and each day as none arrived, he began to feel that perhaps his resoluteness in the face of their opposition had triumphed and that maybe they had abandoned their plans and would leave him alone.

He gave interviews to the local press and a photograph appeared of the defiant local hero standing in front of his shop window in which was displayed a large Union Jack. He was featured for almost a week, elevated in their columns, as something of an epic fighter, a traditionalist, a rugged individualist, until instructions were handed down from some higher authority and his case was suddenly dropped. But the publicity of even a short week opened up new dimensions for Ted. Old ladies stopped him in the street and shook his hand. And though local traitors no longer had anything to do with him, for the most part because they were too preoccupied with thoughts of investing their recently acquired windfalls and enjoying a sense of liberation from the white elephants that had been theirs for so long, merchants in others parts of the town were only too willing to embrace Ted's cause and he was invited on several occasions to address their meetings. His message was simple, the voice of the small shopkeeper, of free enterprise. He hinted darkly at the way trade unions were holding the country to ransom, driving up prices with their excessive wage demands. 'And who suffers?' he went on, flushed with his new-found rhetorical skills. 'The small man who provides a service, who makes available to the public those essential items, food, clothing, consumer goods. And what other conspiracies are there afoot to divest us of our birthright? Large monopolies run by the swarthy, the black, the foreign.' He concluded with all the pained authority of one who knew from bitter experience. They cheered him as he sat down, and when the chairman suggested that he should enter the local political arena he blushed with modest pride.

It was at the crest of this wave that his hopes were dashed by a small brown envelope that arrived one Monday morning by the first post. It came from the Town Council and advised him that steps were now under way to compulsorily purchase his property. He recoiled in despair at the impersonal style and its mealy-mouthed typeface, but let the functionaries come with their demands, he would still defy them. Ever more resolute, he drove to the Town Hall and demanded an audience with the town planner. They stalled him with excuses that Mr Bromley was not at that moment available, that he was in conference, that should he, Mr Hardin, care to reveal the subject matter of his enquiry it would be duly passed on. But Ted was in no mood for dealing with mere intermediaries. His words were only for the ears of the planner himself and he insisted on an appointment with such force that the bewildered and timid Miss Harris, secretary of the planner for all of fifteen years, capitulated and entered into her boss's diary in her neat round handwriting an appointment for the following Thursday.

Ted arrived early, militant, resolute, and one glance into the face of Alec Bromley revealed all the shifty and underhand treachery that had gone on behind his back. He said, 'What's the meaning of this?' waving the order in his hand.

Alec looked at some papers on his desk and said, 'I'm afraid it means exactly what it says, Ted.'

'But what right do you have to do this?'

'The right invested in me and the committee. We convened and discussed and we consider that it's in the town's best interest to effect a compulsory purchase order.'

'I'll take you to court.'

'The order is from the court, Ted, to you. You have a right to state your case to the judge, but I'm telling you, Ted, you don't have a leg to stand on.'

'I see,' said Ted, silenced by the other's authority.

Alec went on, more softly, 'Why don't you take it on the chin? It's not such a tragedy and you have everything to gain.'

But these were not the words that Ted wanted to hear, having listened to them ad nauseam for the past few months, and he got up abruptly from the hard wooden chair that he had been sitting on. He wanted to get out of this room with its drab council-issue office furniture, its worn piece of carpet and its cream walls. He heard the rattling of tea cups outside, and anxious to avoid the humiliation of supping with this new devil, made for the door and with the warning, 'I shall see a solicitor,' opened it and almost knocked over Miss Harris and her tray in his haste to leave.

But no local solicitor would take his case, so hopeless did they think it, and Ted began to despair. He could, of course, go to London and find himself an expensive legal adviser, but he held really little hope of success, so emphatic had been the local advice. The little brown court order had become the ball and chain of a life sentence.

Despairing of legal channels, it occurred to him to try Adler again and it was this line of reasoning that had directed him finally to my flat, where he sat, so nervous and desperate.

I listened with due attentiveness and with a sinking feeling, as much at the thought of my own unwanted and enforced involvement in the whole squalid business as at his plight. More of a shock I suppose was the knowledge of the ruthless methods of my former school chum and current employer. I was not eager to demonstrate partisanship for either side, however, for the excesses that the crisis had revealed or created in Ted's mind were certainly not to my liking, and I would have been happier, I will admit, merely left to the pleasure of my recently acquired stereo earphones. But, alas, Ted's shrill insistence and pleadings for my assistance made that alternative an impossibility, so reluctantly I agreed to do my best to dissuade David Adler from his purposes, promising, however, little hope of success. It seemed, though, to calm Ted's anxiety markedly, and for the first time that evening he almost relaxed and accepted my offer of a large glass of Justerini and Brooks whisky, another taste I had acquired of late. He gulped it down with the speed of someone who had spent several dry and thirstless days in the wilderness. He drank still another large glass and, his tongue now loosened by the effects of alcohol, began muttering such extreme threats against his adversary and the world at large that I became alarmed for my own safety, convinced that his heady diatribe against the multifarious conspiracies abroad in the land included my own good self. I managed at length to steer him towards the door and down to his car, into which I hurriedly pushed him, hoping that he would not discover the large scratch mark that had been scored into his paint-work, doubtless by the local juvenile vandals. Fortunately his sight was fixed on higher and headier points, and after several attempts with the ignition key and an over-indulgence of choke, he jerked off into the dim Paddington streets, the defacement undetected.

But he had left me with a predicament, one which I was reluctant to grapple with. I spent a restless night, weighing the pros and cons as objectively as I could, and when finally sleep embraced me I had come to the tentative conclusion that I might casually mention the subject to David Adler on the morrow.

Which I did. I made my way to his surprisingly modest and undemonstrative suite of offices off Bond Street, hesitated only briefly on the pavement, and entered. The atmosphere within was charged to say the least, and I had the impression of the kind of determined expectancy that must precede the opening of a battle. Telephones were ringing, clerks were scurrying, there were departures and arrivals, and amidst all at his panoramic desk sat the mastermind himself, playing patience rather irritably.

He looked up as I came through the door and nodded a perfunctory greeting. 'We're a bit busy at the moment,' he said, returning to his cards.

'Oh well, perhaps I'd better go away.'

'Well, you obviously came for something. What is it?'

It did not seem to me to be a favourable atmosphere in which to advance the case of Ted Hardin, but as he was sitting now half attentively I had to grasp the opportunity as it had rendered itself. I began hesitantly at first, for indeed I questioned my perogative in this matter, but once I had launched into my plea, it seemed churlish to abandon it. I said, 'The man is obviously in a terrible state. He's bitterly disappointed at the prospect of the loss of his livelihood and his property. Surely there must be a more human way of dealing with these matters. I don't personally like the man, but he is deserving of a certain sympathy and perhaps he has been harshly treated.'

I finished and a silence fell on the room, finally broken by a sigh from David. He turned up one more card before saying, 'Have you finished?'

To which I replied I had.

Then he looked at me with a withering and tired expression, his head cocked to one side, and said, 'Why don't you mind your own fucking business?'

And before I could reply, perhaps fortunately, for an answer had not entered my head, the telephone rang and he picked up the receiver, said 'yuh' twice and left the room.

When he returned about five minutes later he was all smiles. 'Well, old son,' he said with an East End familiarity, 'it's all set up. Pop round tomorrow and we'll have a drink. The demolition gangs move in in the morning.'

Chapter 15

Like some grotesque version of bar skittles, the mobile crane lurched and sent a huge heavy ball on the end of a chain swinging into the wall of the building. The brick face cracked on impact, at first sending to the ground some bricks and plaster but giving the impression that it was strong enough to sustain further shock, till a second thudding swing burst through the wall and with a dull rumble the top swayed and tottered for a split second before cascading downwards in an explosion of swirling brick and plaster. Relentlessly the ball swung again and again, pummelling the wall like some incensed mechanical punchdrunk heavyweight. It swung, bang, and down went the wall, bang and more rafters shattered and slumped to the floor. In time the whole shop was brought to its knees, a heap of rubble and concrete and brick and plaster and wood, that the bulldozers with their thuggish iron jaws scooped victoriously away. When the dust cleared you could see lying pathetically on the ground a cracked sign, 'Hardin's'.

He watched it as though his own body was being beaten, felt every blow in a stunned pained silence. Everything that he had built his adult life on was in ruins, his plans, his ambitions, his innovations, his improvements, lying there like so much bomb damage. He noticed neither his tears, nor his clothes and face that were streaked with the powder of plaster. He just stood there, as close as the workmen would allow for his safety, and even after the site had been cleared, and the crane moved on to claim yet another victim, he remained there motionless, like a still photo of a stunned and half-crazed tramp.

Only his mind was moving like an uncontrolled thing that flooded with memories of the past, of all that he had stood for, and the torrent in which they came made yet more painful the present moment of nothingness. And at that point of his great desolation came a new thought with all the sudden sharp clarity of a vision. Passers-by who saw his comic figure, stained and tattered, stared and tried to hear the mumblings that moaned from his lips. One kindly soul stopped to ask if he was all right, but the words fell on stony ears and the eyes that stared fixedly ahead saw nothing.

Most gave him a passing glance before moving on.

But had they known that at nine o'clock some inner voice was speaking to him in such imperative tones that he could only obey for his life, had they understood, seen him nod his head in agreement and approval of the silent instructions that were so detailed and worked out, then perhaps they might have checked him as he hurried suddenly from the scene of desolation, and prevented him from getting into his car and driving off towards London.

It was our third bottle of champagne and still he was insisting how clever he was, and still she leant over to kiss him as if to prove his claim each time. And then he would laugh to himself and pat me on the knee and say, 'You know, George, the trouble with you is you're a mug. I've liked you, but I've always thought you were a mug. You know what I stand to make out of this deal? A cool million. And do you know what that means? That's better than all the fairy godmother's wands that they used to wave at the pantos. It's real magic. There's nothing you can't turn it into. Nothing it won't do.'

It is not the sort of assertion than can be satisfactorily replied to in this world, so I merely smiled and nodded my head in a sort of reluctant agreement.

'But what about love?' said I knowingly.

Of a sudden I felt a terrible fatigue. There is indeed something so wearisome about this world in which these cheap, banal, oft-reiterated remarks have such currency, for money, a handful of notes, is the driving spring that forces all our dances. Our lives are variations on a theme, but when will life become the theme itself? In the six months I had been involved with this man, had watched a broken, bored, desperate woman flower and yet, in that flowering, lose the charm that she already had. Her clothes were now more expensive, the plastic surgeon had reshaped her nose, her hair was done by the best hairdressers, but so what? Can our dreams be so easily bought? Does money merely provide the gateway to living out all the dross of illusion that we gather and garner in our youth? Oh for a muse of fire to scorch and wither each cheap desire! In my role of jester and go-between I too was several pounds the richer.

I got up to leave but he grabbed my arm and said, 'Where are you going, George? This is a celebration.'

'I'm tired,' I said. 'I need some sleep.'

'And sleep, George, you shall have. The guest room is all yours.'

'No, no. I'll go home.'

'No, you stay. You can take Maureen to the races tomorrow. I insist.'

I suppose nothing would have been simpler than to walk out of the door, but I did not. I began to feel this man had some terrible spell over me, and I found myself in the spare room, he patting my shoulder. 'You know, what you need is a woman, George. I'll fix one up for you.'

It was senseless to argue.

I lay in bed, but sleep kept eluding me in some maddening way. A thousand minor irrelevances crowded my head, questions buzzing like flies, and when at last I seemed to drift off some nagging waking part warned me, and conscious of it I woke. I don't know how long I tossed and turned there, maybe an hour, but with a throat now parched and that sluggish let-down hangover that champagne gives, I got up from the bed in search of water.

There was a basin in the wall, part of a wardrobe fixture, and above the basin a cupboard which was ajar, and often I wonder whether it had been left in that position deliberately. At all events I opened it in search of a glass.

It is difficult to describe the scene that met my eye. I thought at first that some trick of vision had afflicted me, tired and part-conscious as I was, but it was no hallucination. Time confirmed it, and with the confirmation I began to wonder whether I was visible to them, but a moment's thought led me to the conclusion that I stood in front of a two-way mirror that made me invisible.

Framed by the outline of the cupboard itself, it was as if I watched a silent blue movie, for before me in all its mirrored shapes was the bedroom of David. He was naked, prostrate on his knees as if begging, while above him stood Maureen, clad in boots and those scant gauzy knickers, holding in her hand a riding switch. A supplicant, he buried his face in her crotch, his arms clasped round her thighs, but she, stern and reproachful of his desires, was beating him across the back.

I watched it dumbstruck, trembling, then turned away. But something made me look back, some awful lurking, primitive desire of the voyeur. I had to look from the concealing security of the two-way glass at his dread secret, he the dynamic impresario, the cool millionaire, on his knees in a grotesque charade. And what of me? Was I not merely fulfilling the role that I had opted for in life, the heavy breather on the side lines.

What followed could have seemed to be merely comic, something out of a Keystone Cops picture, but with the sudden reversal of a Hitchcock suspense thriller. I noticed him first reflected in a mirror. In fact I saw him before they did. He looked wild, dishevelled, his clothes and face covered in white dust. At first I did not recognise him as Ted. He held an automatic pistol in his left hand.

His lips moved. I could hear nothing, but they sprang apart and she must have screamed. Knowing Maureen, it was probably more out of embarrassment and shame than fear, though fear could not have been long in coming, for the look in Ted's eyes and the way he menaced them with his gun could only cause terror.

David looked alarmed, but it was only momentary, for soon he was attempting to negotiate with his familiar charm and persuasiveness. He walked over to Ted, his face hidden from my view. In response, Ted pointed the gun at his genitals and fired. The report cracked one of the mirrors.

I tried to move, but my legs were paralysed, without feeling. I was merely a prisoner of this spectacle, unable to intervene.

Maureen started to scream, a ghastly soundless silent-movie scream, while Ted advanced on her. When he got to touching distance – she was sobbing and pleading with him by now – he pushed her onto the bed. Then, placing the barrel of the pistol into her vagina, he fired twice.

At that point I must have fainted.

Ted was certified by the courts as insane. I was required to testify as witness. At the police station I gave evidence and explained my paralysis. When they finally let me go I overheard, as I was meant to overhear, a sergeant say, 'Paralysis. If I had my way I'd kick him so hard he'd be paralysed for life.'

The newspapers paid a certain amount of attention to the case, though many of the details were perforce hushed up.

It was considered that silence was the best policy for all concerned.

On the Stock Market the shares of Adler Enterprises fell several points at the news, but when it was announced that business would of course continue, at the direction of the board, they returned to their usual figure.

In Trowbridge Spa an eighteen-storey structure now dominates the new town centre development. It is named Millennium Towers. It is as yet unoccupied and stands there, at times reflecting the sunlight in each of its thousand windows, emptily and profitably, waiting for rent values to rise.

On the Typeface

This book is set in Electra, a typeface designed by William Addison Dwiggins for use on Linotype typesetting machines in 1935. Dwiggins, a mildly eccentric book designer, illustrator, calligrapher and creator of marionettes, is credited with coining the term 'graphic design'.

Dwiggins's foray into type design began with a challenge from the Mergenthaler Linotype Company, after he had criticized the dearth of usable san serifs. Electra was Dwiggins's first type design for book setting and would be one of his most enduring.

While the popular book faces of his time were revivals of fifteenth- and sixteenth-century printing types, Dwiggins sought to create a typeface that reflected the modern environment. As his friend and fellow illustrator Rudolph Ruzicka commented, Electra was 'the crystallization of [Dwiggins's] own calligraphic hand'. Its unbracketed serifs, flat arches, and open counters make for a face mild in pretence but alive in personality. Dwiggins explained, 'The weighted top serifs of the straight letters of the lower case: that is a thing that occurs when you are making formal letters with a pen, writing quickly. And the flat way the curves get away from the straight stems: that is a speed product.'